GILL JEPSON

Gill Jepson

OUT OF TIME 3

The Cistercian Conspiracy

By the same author

Out of Time – The Secret of the Swan
Out of Time 2 – Raven's Hoard
Guy the Grumpy Gargoyle

GILL JEPSON

OUT OF TIME 3

The Cistercian Conspiracy

Matador
9 Priory Business Park,
Wistow Road
Kibworth Beauchamp
Leicester LE8 0RX, UK
Tel: (+44) 116 279 2299
Fax: (+44) 116 279 2277
Email: books@troubador.co.uk
Web: www.troubador.co.uk/matador

ISBN 978 1784620 554

British Library Cataloguing in Publication Data.
A catalogue record for this book is available from the British Library.

Typeset in 11pt Palatino by Troubador Publishing Ltd, Leicester, UK
Printed and bound in Great Britain by TJ International, Padstow, Cornwall

Matador is an imprint of Troubador Publishing Ltd

*For Harry and our three wonderful children
and remembering Alice Leach*

CHAPTER 1

RESCUE

The mobile was ringing. He looked at the screen. Nate. What did he want? It continued to ring.

"Yeah? Whadda ya want?" Rob snapped briskly.

"Can you do me a favour?"

He sighed. "Depends… what is it?"

"I need you to get me a McDonalds… for three…"

"D'ya think I'm made of money? Why can't you get it?"

"Erm… it's a long story. Look, I'll pay you back… and I need a lift too."

"For God's sake! I'm not your slave y' know? Where are you?"

"Abbot's Wood… there are three of us… we need a lift to Rampside… but bring three Big Macs will ya?"

He considered for a second. He wasn't doing much. Suppose he could.

"Ok, I'll see you on the road outside Abbot's Wood in fifteen minutes."

He sped off to Hollywood Park. What an odd choice of name for a retail park. You half expected a glamorous American style mall… not a Bowling Alley, a Comet and a Curry's. He wondered which town councillor had kept that little joke up his sleeve. He skidded into the drive-through at McDonalds, as usual misjudging the corner. After buying the food he raced off again, along Abbey Road towards Abbot's Wood. What did his kid brother think he was doing? He had always been quirky – but recently he had taken quirky to a whole new level. Bad enough that he chose to hang out in fields grubbing about in the ground looking for artefacts, but recently he had even brought home a skull. The old guy who ran the dig had died and left him a skull! Rob could have understood if he had left a coin or some pottery – but a skull? That was just perverse. He had teased his brother and that had caused a massive uproar with everyone yelling and the skull had been banished to the shed.

He didn't know what sort of strangeness was going on, but the back garden had been trashed by vandals in the night and Nate had been very edgy about it all. So had Rebecca his kid sister – sometimes wondered if he actually was related to those two at all. Then later the next morning, he had had to come back home to get his shin pads for a five-a-side match he was playing in. The house was empty – everyone was out, except Nate. He was in the garden, he never saw Rob as he went upstairs to get the pads. He couldn't resist looking through the window at Nate to see what he was doing. He had expected to see him sunbathing; but no – not his brother! He was digging and laying patio flags. Trying to curry favour with his dad he thought, until he saw the box with the skull inside. The idiot was burying it. What was the point in that? Surely, it had already been in the ground – so why bury it again? He was going to shout down some abuse, but then he noticed a massive black raven perched on the hedge. It was crowing and it stared straight at his brother as if it approved. He shuddered. It unnerved him a little. It seemed to herald something strange and mysterious.

Then for the last week nobody had seen hide or hair of him because he was camping out somewhere and now he was up at the abbey again. Most of all… who were the nutters he was hanging round with this time? His array of strange friends was legendary, so he was prepared for anything. Almost.

He drew to a sudden halt at the small lay-by near the entrance to Abbot's Wood. There they were. Three weirdos. What… the… heck… were they dressed in? Weir – dos! They looked like extras from some boring historical drama on the BBC. Embarrassing. The girl looked like she was about to pass out or something and the bloke – well, he just looked ridiculous, dressed up like a highwayman. What *was* his brother doing with these freaks?

Nate bundled the couple into the back, they both looked too terrified to move.

"You are seriously weird! What do you wanna do all this re-enactment stuff for?" Rob laughed.

"It's to help people get the idea of the past," replied Nate.

"All of you going then?" he said nodding to the others.

"Er – yeah! They're with me," said Nate, "Did ya get the Maccies?"

"Doh! What do you think this is?" Rob said, lifting two brown bags from the well of the front seat as Nate got in. "And watch the drinks... don't knock 'em over!" he instructed.

They sped off towards Yarlside at an alarming rate of knots, Rob keeping up speed to the beat of the music. A small whimper escaped from Dolly's mouth. He glanced in the rear view mirror at the two in the back.

"You're all freaks! And do you have to look so filthy? I'm sure they had soap in the eighteenth century!" he chuckled.

"I wouldn't bet on it Rob! But you wouldn't know!"

"Anyway you owe me for the McDonald's and my petrol," Rob insisted. "You back tomorrow? Mum was asking... she said you've gotta tidy your room before school on Monday."

Nate's eyebrows raised in surprise.

"What day is it today?" he laughed nervously.

"Plonker! It's Thursday... you dim or what?" retorted Rob. What was this kid on?

"I forgot... it seems centuries since I was home," he quipped, smiling.

"No, you've only been camping since Monday, but Mum wants you back Saturday," added Rob with authority.

Rob drew to a halt at the car park next to the Concle Inn. Nate got out and grabbed the bags of food and the drinks. The two reluctant passengers scrambled out of the back seat and stood on the gravel. Dolly dropped a small curtsey in thanks for the end of the journey and Rob shook his head in disbelief.

"Freaks!" Rob muttered, as he pulled away and sped off down the road back to Barrow. What was that all about? Nate was becoming obsessed with this history stuff. It couldn't be healthy. He caught sight of them in the rear view mirror, walking towards the beach. His view was impeded by a hazy cloud of sand or dust. Within moments they were shrouded from view and it was the last he saw of them.

Chapter 2

Barrow village 1846

The young man surveyed the site. It was a paltry little place, very backward and old fashioned. It was nothing like Bolton where he came from. The villagers had hardly heard of the railway. Well he would change that. He and the Furness Railway Company! The whole place would be unrecognisable in a few years, he knew what he was capable of and this place would remember him forever. He watched from a distance as they laid more track, the precision was amazing and he was pleased to be responsible for the execution of the new railway. He sat down on the grass on top of Rabbit Hill and surveyed the view across the sea. A small rabbit hopped and skipped in front of him, disappearing into a burrow in the hillside. That explained the stupid name then? He smiled knowingly.

Below him at the foot of the hill was the beginning of the extension of the Furness Railway. He envisioned the new station and the offices, which would be built there and looked at the tiny village to the north, a few meagre cottages, farms and an inn or two. It nestled in the dip between two hills, cradled beside the lapping waters of a small tidal channel. The channel was sectioned off by small piers and yards, where the slate and iron ore were loaded. The railway delivered the unprocessed rock to the yards and then it was shipped out to foundries far afield to be made into metal. Soon the link would extend beyond Barrow and take the ore out and bring more miners in.

He gazed across the water to the small island, inhabited only by one family, in an ostentatious house named after them, Michaelson House. He would have a house like that one day. No… he would have a bigger one… much bigger. Beyond Barrow Island sat the larger Walney Island curled around the peninsula like large protective arms. It was cut off for so many hours a day and the farmers over there were isolated at certain times of the year and arranged their days to suit the tides. It was not part of his plan, with no bridge it was useless to him and would probably remain a rural backwater.

He sank back into the grass, put his arms behind his head and closed his eyes. He reflected on his good luck in being charged to undertake this job by the Directors of the railway. He still had a lot to prove, but knew he could show them what he was made of. He smiled to himself when he remembered the day they had landed the first engine. The villagers had turned out to look at the great beast, standing in groups and chatting. They watched patiently as the locomotive was unloaded from the barge and as the engineers put it into working order. He was amused at their reaction when the huge machine burst into life, hissing, spitting and steaming like some angry mythical creature. Many of the bystanders screamed and hollered, some running for cover, others hiding behind walls and trees, unable to comprehend its sudden animation. Its unholy noise and plume of steam and smoke was more than most could stand. They had to be calmed down and reassured like children. James could not believe it, in Bolton where he had been born modern inventions were not held in such awe and terror. He would make sure that the villagers of Barrow would learn to embrace these machines, and learn to love them, just as he did himself.

He had a dream. It was a dream, which would revolutionise the village of Barrow. He knew that it was ripe for picking! Slate was brought down from the quarry at Kirkby and Lord Burlington had the foresight to create the Furness Railway. Next there would be exploration to find more iron ore, as soon as that was found the industry could grow. He for one would be right at the front when the 'industrial revolution' finally hit Barrow.

Chapter 3

The monk

Rob dragged the heavy chocolate brown Labrador down the lane, he didn't know why he had to take a turn walking the dog, after all, he hadn't wanted a dog. He actually liked Sam, but he loved to stop and sniff every blade of grass, so a short walk took forever and he had other things to do. The good thing was he could at least have some thinking time and go over his news stories in his head. He was on a work placement at the local newspaper and it had been an interesting and busy summer so far.

He hauled the reluctant dog towards Bow Bridge and narrowly missed being knocked down by a car, because Sam halted in the middle of the lane. He pushed him through the gate and let him off the lead. The Labrador bounced across the grass, aiming straight for the river. Mum would not be pleased if the dog went home muddy and wet. The huge dog splashed and jumped joyously in the little beck, he was in his element and Rob knew it was going to be a difficult task to get him out again.

Ah well… no point worrying now. Rob sauntered along the river bank following the daft dog as he gambolled along the fast flowing beck towards the railway line. He was quite funny to watch… not a care in the world and oblivious to everything else. Suddenly, the dog stopped dead in his tracks, the water lapping around his legs, a low growl escaped from his curled lips and every sinew was as taut as a bowstring. Rob was shocked because Sam was a placid and friendly dog and it was unusual for him to react aggressively. Rob looked around to see what the dog was looking at. Someone was walking slowly on the brow of the hill towards the abbey, but he couldn't see him clearly. The dog had jumped out of the water and was now standing close to Rob's legs. He was alert and still growling beneath his breath.

"Come on you dozy dog!" Rob said as he slipped the lead back onto the dog's collar. "There's nothing to be scared of…"

They walked slowly towards the railway line and the level crossing. Rob was a bit reluctant about going this way in case the dog stopped again, he checked the lights and looked into the tunnel and there was no sign of a train. He thought it was safe to go and pulled the dog quickly across the footbridge. When they had reached the other side he struggled to negotiate their way through the heavily sprung wooden gate. He was engrossed in pulling the dog through when he suddenly jumped. The dog growled and yelped and Rob took a sharp breath, his arms prickling. He had almost bumped into another person. He hadn't heard him approach and he was surprised. Rob took a step back and tried to pull the dog away.

Sam was now on his hind legs, straining to get off

the lead and growling and barking noisily. Rob heaved at the lead and tightened his grip. He hadn't had chance to look at the person properly and was unable to understand Sam's reaction. The man was tall and thick set, he peered at him with steely eyes. His severe sharp nose gave him the appearance of a very hungry vulture and he sniffed as though he was assessing whether he would be worthy prey.

"Your brother is mixing with the wrong people. You must warn him that if he continues in this way he will only come to grief."

Rob looked blankly at him. What was he going on about? How did he know he *had* a brother?

"The young man will court trouble if he does not cease his efforts to steal my treasure!"

Again, a blank expression. The dog was going wild and it was all Rob could do to keep him under control. His heart fluttered, he wanted to run, but his path was blocked by this crazy man – was he really talking about Nate? What on earth had he got himself into?

"Dunno what you're talking about mate! I'm just out for a walk… me dad's over there, so let me past."

The man smirked. He glanced arrogantly to left and right, demonstrating that he knew Rob was alone. Behind him, just off the road, through the trees, a black car purred to a halt. A youth, another man and a middle-aged woman were inside. At first Rob thought he could call to them for help, but then the youth jumped out and it was evident that he was this man's companion. Rob was shaking and was almost ready to let Sam go and do his worst. Just when he thought things could be no worse, something happened which was even more bizarre. Behind the man a grey mist began to emerge. The air became still and then was filled with an electrical charge, which crackled crisply. From within the mist a figure appeared.

The man shuddered. The few hairs on his balding pate stood on end as though he had stuck his fingers in an electrical socket. Behind him a monk had emerged, draped in a white habit, topped with a black scapula and cowl. Rob nearly passed out. However, the man looked none too pleased either. Sam yelped but lay flat to the ground, eyes fixed on this apparition. The man cursed and made his way through the vegetation to the side of the lane where the vintage black Wolsley car was waiting, engine vibrating quietly. He got into the passenger seat, slammed the door and the car revved speedily away.

By now Rob was sweating, glad that the crazy man had left but now what? A ghost? His common sense told him it could not be, but he had to believe his own eyes. The dog was now whining, as scared as he was himself. The monk smiled benignly and gave him the sign of blessing, but Rob was rooted firmly to the spot. When he got hold of his kid brother he would…

"'Tis not thy brother's fault my son," said the monk softly, as though he had read his thoughts.

Rob's mouth gaped open… what the…

"Thy brother is in great danger and thou must beware of those who threaten the abbey and its treasure," he smiled again, almost hypnotically. Rob began to feel more at ease and his muscles relaxed allowing him to breathe freely again.

"I don't know what you're talking about... " he whispered huskily.

"Thou shalt in good time, my son, the time will come when thou must assist thy brother to save a precious treasure and seek out another thyself.... the time *will* come and ye will be in grave danger..."

Before Rob could ask more the monk began to evaporate before his eyes, becoming transparent and finally disappearing completely, leaving behind blue crackling energy. His mouth was open ready to ask all kinds of questions, but it was too late. He shivered; both he and the dog became intent in moving quickly through the coppice onto the pavement that followed the perimeter of the abbey. As he walked swiftly around the abbey he noticed Mr Mason, working on the foundations in the lay brother's frater. The old chap waved reassuringly and Rob called over to him, saying hello.

Behind him, one... two... and then three magpies swooped silently down onto the railings beyond, unobserved by Rob, but registered by Mr Steele, the English Heritage supervisor, who was standing, sinisterly silent in the archway to the church. Steele watched them for a few minutes and then slid quietly away, ruminating on this new problem. How many more of these irritating brats would he have to deal with? He would need to contact Silas, his cousin; they must not lose sight of the treasures now!

Chapter 4

Divine Intervention

The abbey rose up, a magnificent pile of crumbling red sandstone; it was an impressive edifice. Unfortunately, there was no option, it would have to go! There must be no sentiment in business – that, he knew. James had already looked at the terrain of the prospective route of the track to the east and it would add unnecessary cost and effort to the project if they tried to avoid it. After all, nobody really came here; the local people took it for granted – surely nobody would object to its destruction. They certainly didn't cry out when the old King got rid of it in the first place.

Yet in his heart a glimmer of a concern flickered. Was it right to destroy this amazing place? He could not fail to appreciate its beauty, nor could he ignore its calm and its silence and spirituality. He knew that one of the engineers; Mr MacLean had grave reservations and constantly piped up in meetings with the Directors. No, MacLean would have to change his mind too, nothing could divert his plan, and it had to go forward. After all it avoided going through the hill and would be considerably cheaper to demolish the old abbey. It would cost almost three hundred pounds to blast a tunnel through the substantial hillside and the Earl would not be pleased if costs rose again. He already regarded the new railway as a nuisance and a drain on his resources, despite it being an essential part of the plan to industrialise Barrow-in-Furness.

James sat on the grassy hill rolling down towards the main church. He leaned back on his elbows and surveyed the scene, bathed in warm sunlight. It was close and his eyelids drooped. He dozed momentarily and basked in the warmth like an exotic plant in a greenhouse. He was overcome with a heavy drowsiness and he revelled in daydreaming about his great plans for the future. His reverie was disturbed by a cool, dark shadow falling across him. He blinked and covered his eyes with his hand against the bright sunshine. A tall silhouette was bathed in the golden aura of the sun and rose above him powerfully. James was unable to make out who it was; he assumed it was one of the local labourers. He sat up abruptly and looked more closely at the figure in front of him. His blood ran cold and his heart stopped dead in his chest.

The figure became clear and James was as still as one of the abbey carvings. He was incredulous – he knew what he was seeing was impossible. It was madness! Was this the result of sunstroke? Whatever it was, it certainly could not be what he saw before him now. A monk? Ridiculous! There were no monks living at this abbey anymore!

"My son," a velvety voice emerged from the solemn monk.

James stared.

"Thou must not lay waste to our proud abbey. It

would be a sacrilege as great as that which has been suffered before."

James gulped and his mouth was dry.

"Thou must discover a better means to transport thy spitting, devilish beast through this valley; thou must not destroy this abbey. Thou *wilt* not destroy this abbey," the monk commanded in cool, dulcet tones.

The monk stood calmly observing the young man, moving not a muscle. His white habit reflected the light of the sun, blinding James with its luminescence. The brightness was so intense that he covered his eyes again. When he uncovered them the spectre had gone.

He remained rooted to the spot as solidly as an old oak tree. His skin was clammy and he shivered involuntarily. He was too shaken to move immediately. Instead, he sat immobile for several minutes, not trusting himself to move. Thoughts popped inside his skull like a delinquent firework and his heart was beating as fast as any steam train. James could not believe that he had seen a medieval monk, it was impossible and against any scientific ideals that he held dear. He must have been hallucinating… or dreaming. The scientist dwelling within him would not allow him to believe what he had seen. Already, he was dismissing the very idea and began inventing rational explanations to allay his fears. He must have had too much sun. Yes, that was it! Sunstroke! He had heard of people becoming delirious with the sun. He comforted himself with the thought and smiled to himself.

He sprang to his feet and brushed the loose stalks of grass from his trousers, picked up his hat and placed it on his head. He walked towards the old cottage by the lane, through the abbey, drinking in every detail as he went. Truly, it was an amazing and beautiful building, but the railway would bring jobs, it would create wealth, it was after all, progress. Who could argue against that? This old pile of stones however, beautiful was an impediment and it had to be overcome. Whether the monk was imagined or ghostly; he would choose to ignore it, nothing must stop his great railway. He would rush back to Barrow and arrange for the Irish labourers to move up the line tomorrow. The plans were laid and nothing would delay them now, not even fevered imaginings. His confidence was bolstered and his determination doubled, all thoughts of what he had seen were pushed deep within his brain, filed away and forgotten. He smiled self-assured and smug. A small lingering doubt fluttered across his mind like a moth searching for candlelight. *Could* he bring in the navvies and their demonic dynamite? Time would tell… but he was running out of that very commodity.

CHAPTER 5

A DISCOVERY

Rob had been mulling over the unsettling events of the afternoon. He was a black and white sort of person. Things were clear-cut in his eyes and that's why becoming a journalist attracted him so much, because you had to provide balance, showing both sides equally. This weird stuff was not something he could understand or believe in. You could not see a fifteenth century monk in the twenty-first century. Once you were dead, that was it. Like switching off a computer. Like Granddad... out like a light. Instantly! His eyes prickled at the thought and he shook himself – telling himself to get a grip.

He let a heavy sigh escape and his eyes fell upon the last picture they had of Granddad, surrounded by his family, those most important to him. His sister had struggled most; she was only young and the whole shocking circumstance of Granddad's sudden death rocked her whole world. However, he reasoned, he and Nate, his brother had known Granddad longer and therefore must miss him more. Whatever! He had gone! End of story.

So what was this monk thing about? He thought it could have been one of Nate's friends dressed up to freak him out… but then how did he manage to disappear so effectively? So what did that leave? A hallucination? Or could it have been a real live (dead) ghost? He couldn't make up his mind whether to be more scared of the monk or the heavies who had tried to accost him. Heavies? What was that all about? Now *that* was weird. Who were they? What did they want? This had to be something to do with his crazy brother, of that he was sure!

He wanted to find his brother and sort him out. Who knew what sort of a mess he had got himself into? He was going to find out, he hadn't been seen again for days and he would need to be forced to admit to whatever ridiculous scheme he had become involved in.

Rob was down at Baycliff at teatime, working at the Fisherman's Arms as a waiter. If he went down a bit earlier he could catch hold of Nate at Aldingham as he drove through. He slowed down at the field, which housed Aldingham motte and could see some of the string and canes, which Nate had measured out to do his field survey. He could see the little blue tent that Granddad had bought him but not a sign of the boy himself. Rob pulled in to the grass verge by the gate and peeped the horn to attract his attention. There was no movement. He certainly wasn't going to trek across the muddy field in his work clothes. Mr Haynes, his boss was very particular about his waiting on staff and how they looked. Rob was careful to ensure that his shirt was fresh and white and his shoes were polished, he was proud of his role and had even learnt the considerable skills of silver service. He peered across the field but could see no trace.

He tapped his fingers impatiently on the steering wheel, wondering what to do next. He had a flash of inspiration. Nate might be down at the church. He often went poking around churches and graveyards; Rob shook his head involuntary. He would never understand his brother in a million years. It took two minutes to drive down to the old church hunkered at the edge of the beach at Aldingham. As he drew into the small car park he noticed some children on their bikes racing up the hill. He squinted and tried to see more clearly. He realised with surprise that it was Rebecca his sister and her friends. He got out of the car and tried to shout to them but they were too far away to hear. He shrugged and turned to the church to go and look for Nate. As he walked towards the gate he noticed a young boy sitting on the wall. He nodded in acknowledgement and continued walking towards the church.

"There's nobody in the church," the boy offered.

Rob turned to look at him. Bemused, he surveyed the young lad, dressed in old-fashioned, knee-length grey shorts, a jersey and a cap. He looked… odd… and what *did* he have on his feet? A pair of… clogs! He stared rudely at the lad's strange attire and as he lifted his gaze he met his eyes. The boy grinned widely and winked.

"I said… there's nobody in the church!" he repeated emphatically.

"Yeah, I heard you thanks," Rob answered, a little irked at the lad's cheek.

"Just saying… you're looking fer someone aren't you?"

Rob halted.

"Yeah… my brother… You seen him? He's fair haired, bit shorter than me… bit of a scruff and hangs round with some right weirdos."

The boy let out a hearty chuckle.

"Nope… not seen him… not today!"

Something about this kid was familiar. Rob studied him more closely. The twinkling blue eyes, full of fun, the broad grin, the rather large ears that stuck out just a little bit too much… and that deep infectious chuckle… he couldn't put his finger on it.

"You a mate of my sister Rebecca? I just saw her riding up the lane… were you with her? I hope you haven't been leading her into trouble… I've enough to worry about with my brother…" he trailed off.

The boy's sincere gaze unnerved him. His brow knitted with confusion. What was it that worried him about this boy?

"I haven't done anything… don't worry, nobody will harm her, not while I'm around," he said. "Anyway, got to go and get my tea – it's a long ride back to town," he beamed disarmingly. He turned to get on an old battered bike, which was propped up against the wall. It looked ancient and had a basket at the front, not exactly state of the art.

"While you're around? And what use do you think you'll be… you're a puny little shrimp!" taunted Rob, laughing.

The lad laughed and rode off slowly.

"You're right… in fact they call me *Titch* at home… but I'm stronger than I look and I'll do anything to look after…" his final words were muffled as he turned to face the direction he was going in.

With that he was gone, disappearing into the distance.

What was that he said? "He'd do anything to look after… family"… no that couldn't be right, he must have misheard. He wasn't related, he would know if they were. He hadn't a clue who he was… what sort of name was Titch? The only person he knew who had been called Titch was Granddad; when he was a kid, because he was so small, not that he had really believed him – because he certainly wasn't small as an adult.

He opened the car door and suddenly he felt a trickle of sweat run down his back making him shudder. The hairs on the back of his neck and arms stood on end and he could feel the blood slowly drain from his veins. The realisation of what he had just heard made him nauseous with shock. The frisson of fear made every nerve in his body quiver and seemed to confirm his suspicions. The boy *was* odd and quaintly dressed because he somehow didn't belong, because he was from another time. He was called Titch the same as Granddad… because… he *was* Granddad. Impossible! So, what *was* going on? More weird stuff… a bit too weird… and he still hadn't found Nate. And what about Rebecca? What had all this to do with her? He would bide his time before he mentioned anything, but now… **now**… he was late for work! Typical!

As he drove away from Aldingham he didn't notice a lone magpie take flight from the tree in the churchyard, his black wings beating silently as they propelled him towards the motte.

Chapter 6

Time Tunnel

Rob was worried. It seemed strange that Nate had said nothing to him. Maybe he had been wrong, maybe he had misread everything. Perhaps those guys at the abbey had mistaken him for someone else. He had decided not to mention anything – he didn't want him to think he had gone completely mad. Nate was still camping anyway. Whatever it had been, things had calmed down and returned to normal… almost. He had feelings of doubt and often woke in the morning with heaviness in his head and a squirming sensation in his stomach; it was as if he had all the worries in the world.

He had tried to keep an eye on Rebecca too. He was concerned that she was involved in things she didn't understand. All that stuff with the weird boy – he had decided that it was definitely *not* Granddad… after all how could it be? It was purely coincidence that his nickname was the same. He convinced himself that he had wanted to make the facts fit. He was fiercely protective of his kid sister, especially since Granddad had died. She seemed ok now and she was often hanging out with those friends of hers. So he hadn't spoken to her either – all of which left him feeling a bit useless.

He had been given a small story to cover in his capacity as trainee reporter. His work placement had gone well and the editor, a kindly grandfatherly man, had said he could stay on and would be allowed to cover some of the 'softer' stories. He felt elated – this was what he wanted to do with his life – be a reporter… a really good one too… one who went to dangerous places and really made a difference with his investigative journalism. He knew he had enough determination Granddad had always said he was like a dog with a bone… wouldn't give up, and that's what he would be like with every story.

However, for the moment he would have to be satisfied with the story he was assigned to. It wasn't a terribly exciting one, but maybe he could give it a different twist and make it sound interesting? He had to go to Furness Abbey to cover the special event they were putting on down there. It was a gathering of all kinds of people to support the idea of 'Making Poverty History' ; everyone was meeting at the abbey for a church service. By the time he arrived, with his notepad and camera, people were already congregating. The excitement of the day caught hold and he strode off down the slope into the abbey grounds. In the distance he could see his sister and her friend Megan. The two boys from his street were there too, with the Scouts, the older one was waving to Rebecca. Rob walked past two ladies sitting on a picnic blanket, not realising one of them was his mum. She called out to him and he waved, but carried on – the last thing he wanted was to be caught chatting to his mother when he was on a job.

He sauntered towards the nave of the church, where all the action would be. He passed by Mr Mason who tapped the brim of his English Heritage helmet and smiled. Rob returned the smile and crossed the nave to a low wall, where he sat down. As he did so, he caught sight of another familiar figure. It was that kid… Titch… bold as brass, sitting on a broken column. Rob stood up to make his way across the nave to speak to him, but the lad leapt down from the masonry and ran across to where Rebecca and her friends were. As he watched, it was apparent that there was some sort of problem. A tall, thin man was obstructing them. He pushed his way through the crowds to reach them, but they were too far ahead. They had all run off towards the back of the abbey with the man in hot pursuit. Mr Mason had also appeared and was drawing the children away from the man. As he reached the cloister the crowd thinned and he ran towards the direction they had taken. Without warning a pair of strong hands gripped his shoulders and pulled him back. He struggled and tried to pull away. The hands spun him around and he discovered it was the man who had stopped him in the woods with Sam.

"And where do you think you are going young man?"

"Gerroff! You great ape!" yelled Rob.

"I don't think so… you will stay exactly where you are… you are delving into things which do not concern you!"

"You're mad! I don't know what you're on about," argued Rob pulling himself free momentarily.

The tall balding man lunged at him, but Rob sidestepped him nimbly and then with all his might he pushed the man hard. He overbalanced and fell backwards onto the grass. Without a moment's hesitation he raced along the cloister range and into the undercroft. He sped down towards the infirmary block and caught sight of his sister at the far end of the abbot's house. Mason pointed and the children disappeared from view, he then marched briskly in the other direction. Rob ran back to where the kids had been, he called Mason but he didn't hear him. He ran to the slope, which led down into a drainage tunnel beneath the Abbot's lodgings. Surely, they hadn't gone down there?

He slipped down the banking and landed heavily on his bottom. He was dazed and slid down on his back to the foot of the tunnel. The sun shone into his eyes and for a second his vision was disturbed. A shadow obliterated the light suddenly and then he refocused and saw a figure. He could hear angry voices from afar and knew that his pursuers were looking for him.

"Come on young chap," hissed a voice. "Down here, quickly!"

He followed the instructions and scrambled down the tunnel after the youth.

They ran along, bent double until they reached the opening at the end. They struggled up the slope and out onto the grass. Rob was disorientated and was still wary of his pursuers. He crept to the top of the bank and peered over the wall.

"What are you looking for?" asked the stranger.

"Them! Those guys who were chasing me… and my sister…"

He looked around. Gradually it dawned on him that something was missing. He could not see any trace of his sister and her friends, but he was shocked to see the gathering of people had disappeared too. He slumped to the ground. His brain was arguing with the evidence of his eyes. Where was everyone? He turned to look at his new companion.

A young man in his early twenties stood above him, smiling down thoughtfully. He was slim and of medium height, as his smile faded Rob could tell that he had a serious countenance, there were two small grooves between his eyes, making him look older than he really was. He had brown wavy hair, which flopped over his high forehead, but receded at the sides. Rob thought that one day he would probably be bald. Topping the chestnut coloured hair he had a wide brimmed hat, balanced very carefully at an angle. He had sideburns, which framed his jawline and a distinctive cleft in his chin. His long straight nose gave him an air of importance and his eyes were deep set and piercing, with finely arched brows that gave him an air of constant surprise. He wore a brown jacket and trousers, beneath which he had a shirt with a high collar and waistcoat and an untidy looking black cravat. He reached down and offered his open hand. Rob took it and felt himself pulled to his feet.

Rob dusted himself down and shoved his crumpled notebook and camera into his backpack. He appraised the stranger again. A slow realisation crept over him like dawn creeping over the horizon. This bloke was... from another time... just like that boy. The clothes he wore told the whole story. He was dressed like a Victorian. Something about him told Rob that he wasn't just pretending to be a Victorian, like one those re-enactor friends of Nate – no, there was something genuine, something real about him. The full impact hit him like a punch in the stomach. He felt sick and the colour drained from his cheeks. The young man noticed and looked on with concern.

"Are you quite well? You have a deathly pallor and you look most unwell?"

Even the way he spoke was old fashioned.

"Er yeah, just a bit shocked that's all," Rob responded. That didn't really cover how he felt.

"Well, follow me lad, I have a trap waiting along the lane. I must take you out of reach for the time being..." he grinned, "a few months more and we would be able to take the railway, but we have yet to build the station!"

Rob nodded. He felt dazed as if he was trapped within a dream. He looked around nervously. There seemed little else to do but agree and followed the man across the abbey grounds. He noticed immediately that there were no railings, just a small fence and a track, rather than a road running around the perimeter. The abbey looked different. There was more masonry and lush green ivy adorned the bright red sandstone. He looked towards the nave as they crossed the cloister range. He knew where he was, but was unsure where he was. Everything was confusing and strange and he could not accept that he had travelled back in time. That sort of stuff was his brother's bag, not his.

There was not a sign of the crowd he had left behind. In the distance he could see two young women and an older lady… this was *too* strange. They wore long dresses and bonnets, with parasols placed jauntily over their shoulders, just like in those costume dramas on the telly. As they passed by the ladies the young man doffed his hat and bade them good day. Rob glanced at them and mumbled a similar greeting; they giggled behind their elegantly gloved hands and their mother swiftly guided them away.

As they reached the post where the horse was tethered, still hitched to the trap, the man turned and spoke again,

"I am James by the way… James," Rob waited and half expected him to say Bond… but he didn't, "James Ramsden at your service."

He waited for a similar introduction.

"I'm Rob…" he trailed off, "Why am I here? Why are you here? What's happening?" The questions tumbled out his mouth in a torrent.

"I was told where you would be found and that you were in peril."

"Who told you?"

"Brother John," James replied.

Rob looked blankly.

"The monk… you have seen him I believe?"

His face drained of colour again.

"Ha! I see that you have! I too was nonplussed when he first appeared to me in the abbey."

James unhitched the horse and jumped into the trap, beckoning Rob to join him. He climbed up uncertainly and squeezed onto the narrow seat next to James. They set off with a jolt and the horse clattered off along the uneven road. The contraption was sprung, after a fashion, but it was quite uncomfortable and Rob thought he would not like to travel far in it. They raced along, jolting over every rut and bump in the road, past the Custodian's cottage he knew so well in his time. It looked very different, smoke rose from the chimney and the garden was planted with vegetables, someone actually lived in it. Trees overhung the narrow lane, a green canopy, shading them from the bright sunlight. They drove past Abbot's wood but to his amazement there was no wall, no gatehouse, no driveway, just woodland, wild and unkempt.

They followed the valley past the river, which wound along in an uncontrolled way and there was no railway embankment. Men were working at the far end of the field but he could not see what they were doing. James noticed the direction of his gaze.

"They are preparing the ground for our new branch line – we are to blow a tunnel through the hill behind the abbey. I favoured blowing up the abbey," he laughed.

Rob looked at him in astonishment. Blow up the abbey? Really?

"Ha ha until I met yon monk!" he nodded towards the field, where Rob could make out the still figure of a monk dressed in white in the distance.

He shivered again. James smiled and shrugged.

"You will get used to seeing him after a while! It took me some time to accept that he was not a threat to me... and the railway of course."

"Well, I don't think I'll ever get used to him. He gives me the creeps," replied Rob.

They rattled on through the lane and past Bow Bridge, which was the only recognisable feature. Rob knew they must be travelling towards where he lived in the present, but it was very different. They passed fields and hedgerows and far in the distance he could see the blue glint of the sea. However, many of the familiar landmarks from his time were absent. They drove past the Ship Inn, which was more of a farm house than a public house and on past the Smithy. He had always wondered why the local fish and chip shop was named "The Smithy" – well now he knew – a blacksmith worked at his forge where the chip shop stood in his day. From there onwards Rob was unclear where they were. Everything looked green and rural and there were few recognisable landmarks, he spotted the railway line, newly cut into the landscape. They continued until they reached a small village close to the sea. A narrow channel separated a verdant island from the mainland. Beyond that he espied a larger island and the glint of the Irish Sea beyond that. He assumed from what he saw that he must be in Barrow. He knew it had begun as a small hamlet but had not expected it to be this small. Few of the familiar places had been built yet and it was more rural than the Barrow he knew.

They trotted up a hill, where a lot of building was going on. They arrived at a row of sandstone cottages, glowing pink in the sunlight, newly constructed and the only houses around. He felt he had seen them before and he confirmed this in his head when he noticed a newly built railway station and offices. He glanced at the iron railed wall and the germ of an idea emerged. He was on St George's hill – but as yet there was no St George's church.

James tethered the horse in front of one of the cottages and jumped down, beckoning him to follow. They went inside. This was apparently where James lodged. The small room was sparsely furnished, with a black leaded range along the back wall. A table stood in the middle of the room, covered with a heavy tablecloth, four wooden chairs surrounded it and a rug lay in front of the range. The room was cosy but functional and a few books piled on the cupboard in the alcove were the only indication of any personal belongings.

"Come then… be seated." demanded James, pulling out a chair and pointing to him to sit.

Rob sat.

James disappeared into a small curtained scullery at the back of the cottage and returned with two opaque glasses and a bottle. Rob raised his eyebrows, unsure of what the bottle contained. James poured the brown liquid into the glasses and pushed one towards him. He sniffed the drink first and then tentatively took a sip. It was tingly and sharp… quite refreshing.

"It isn't poison you know! It is the best ginger beer you can find in Barrow."

"Ok I believe you…" Rob smirked at the earnest look on James' face.

"So to work. Brother John tells me that you *must* solve the abbey mystery and find that treasure which is so keenly coveted by your adversaries."

He spoke as though Rob would understand what he was talking about.

Rob winced and ran his fingers through his hair, sighing with exasperation.

"What are you on about? Speak English will you?" He rubbed his eyes as if he was trying to wake up. "What treasure? How does this involve me? I'm not even that interested in the abbey... and more importantly... how do I get home?"

James removed his jacket and hung it on the back of the chair. He sat heavily on the rickety wooden chair opposite Rob and looked directly into his eyes. He seemed to be pondering the predicament hard.

"All I know is that you have to find an important treasure, the loss of which is unthinkable. The monk has appeared to me on many occasions and he has forced me to change my thinking. I too had no great passion for the abbey; indeed my plan would have seen it demolished – but he turned my mind to its great age and importance."

"Well what is it – this treasure?"

"I have no notion I am afraid!"

"Oh well that's brilliant! And how DO I get home?"

James smiled, "I would guess that you will return the way you came. The monk would not have you marooned here and for that matter neither would I!"

"You could be right... I was trying to escape from some people who I didn't like the look of... I suppose you could say he saved my neck. But how did you know I would be at the tunnel?"

"The brother of course, I was surveying and planning where the new station will be and suddenly… there he was. I am used to him now and I listened to what he said and I found you at the other end of the tunnel. Exactly where he said you would be."

Rob's anxiety drained away and he relaxed. His investigative brain began to work overtime. The two young people talked at length and discussed the situation further. Rob discovered that they had much in common – despite the hundred and fifty years which separated them. Both were realists, pragmatic and curious; in another time they might have been friends. They shared with each other the little they knew and Rob was embarrassed by his lack of knowledge. James had been told much by the monk and what he had to tell astounded Rob and gave him food for thought. The tale he told began many years before…

Chapter 7

A Fateful Conspiracy

"'Twas long before my time at the abbey"
Brother John Stell wrote. He was engaged in recording events from the abbey's past and he took his work seriously. Brother John was seated at his place in the Cloister, the summer sun flooding the covered area with a bright and vibrant light; making his task easier than in the dark winter days in the scriptorium. John had been charged with this work and he wrote with great clarity and care. His illuminations were unparalleled in this abbey and probably many others too. Today his thoughts were riddled with worries. He had uncovered a terrible story, which discredited his beloved abbey. It posed another problem too, yet another precious and holy treasure was in need of care.

John's burden was a heavy one and weighed him down daily. He had been entrusted with his guardianship for many years past. His old abbot had passed away many years ago and John had shared his task with only one other person. Robert the Mason was his friend and had braved many dangers to secure and hide the sacred treasures within the abbey. This latest one had been the most difficult to protect and he knew its future safekeeping would be too. He laid down his goose feather quill and stretched his inky fingers for a moment of contemplation. His task from God was a hard one and he sometimes wondered if he was equal to the challenge. He shook his greying head, picked up the quill, dipping it into the ink well carefully, and tapped it to shake off the excess ink. He would be devastated if his work was to be spoiled by a blot… he knew that this was the sin of pride, something he had tussled with since youth. However, he could not help but wish to do a perfect job and his heart gave a joyful leap when he completed an intricate illuminated letter, or finished pages of detailed history. He began to write again.

"When a moste venerable Abbot called Laurens did hold Furnesse in his charge… a terrible plot was woven by his very own bretheren, whom he trusted and loved. Abbot Laurens was a holy and devoted man who ne'er had an ill worde or action against any mann. Furnesse was in those days a place of peace and safety and none would doubt the loyalty of the brothers. Yet sadly three brothers were not true to the abbot, nor to their vowes"

The Vale of Deadly Nightshade in which ye monasterie was nestled held a treachery too horrible to think of. Amongst those holy monks who kept their vowes and followed the sacred rule of St Benedict were the three who defiled the place with their greed, jealousy and vaulting ambition. These kinsmen were discontented with their place in life and plotted to seize great power and riches. They huddled together in the dark shadows of the cloister and conspired to overthrow the abbot and take his place. They had not resolved which one of them would take on the mantle of abbot, but were bent upon his destruction.

The brothers plotted and planned in quiet corners, stealing moments in the cloister, whispering in the warming room or hiding in the herb garden. The Herbarium was close by the infirmarie and the kitchen and was important to their plan. Brother John worked daily and he knew every herbe and plante, which could be used to make unctions, ointments, medicines and possets, those for flavourings and seasoning for food... and those which could be used for ill. Brother John had selected his plant carefully, for it grew in abundance in the low-lying valley. Indeed the Vale of the Nightshade was named for the plant.

Deadly nightshade grew rampantly, amongst the wild garlic and vetch, its deadly nature disguised by its innocent delicate purple beauty. He had learnt his skill well from the old infirmarian. He knew that the poison lay within its roots and that it must be suffused until it made a brew of rich royal red and purple liquor; scentless and deadly. T'would be an easy task; few knew what alchemy went on in the herbarium. The old monk in charge was nearly blind and would not catch sight of the murderous brew...

Brother Andrew prepared to give the poison to the abbot in a most Judas-like way. He was to assist Abbot Laurence at Holy Mass. It would be easy to add the liquid to the chalice, mixed with the holy wine. Abbot Laurence would die quickly and they could then seize power. Or so he had planned.

The conspirators watched anxiously as the abbot began the mass. He looked in rude health and for some time the three monks watched anxiously as he led the prayers. The tension grew, as he seemed to be unharmed by the deadly elixir. It soon became apparent that something was amiss. Beads of sweat glistened on Brother Andrew's brow as he realised that John had miscalculated the dosage of the poison. The service progressed, as though time had halted, every movement the old man made exaggerated and slow. Just as Andrew was about to give up hope, the abbot swayed slightly. He righted himself and drew his hand across his forehead. He swayed again, this time losing his balance and staggered forwards. Brother Andrew looked on eagerly, smiling inwardly as Abbot Laurence leaned forward, clutching at his priestly garments. The old man staggered, falling against the high altar, sending the chalice crashing onto the green glazed tiles of the floor. He stumbled and fell to his knees, disorientated and dizzy, his sight dimming and wavering. His collapse was hidden behind the decorated rood screen, which separated the quire monks from the high altar. Only the Prior and Brother Andrew were with him and they rushed to his aid. He was carried from the church by the monks and taken to his lodgings. He was put to bed, heralding a flurry of activity. The abbot sickened and his skin grew clammy and he had not a vestige of colour in his cheeks.

The guilty monks met in the twilight, their white robes gleaming like ghastly spectres in the gloom. Their voices raised in heated emotion. They knew they risked discovery if the old man recovered and fell to arguing about their course of action.

"What has happened? He is not yet dead!" demanded Brother Andrew. "We will be undone!"

"Thy potion must be too weak… you fool John, we trusted thee to know what thou shouldst do!" snarled Brother Wilfrid.

"'Tis hard to be exact… worry not, I have set more liquor aside if this failed to end his life," he assured.

"And how dost thou think we can reach him now? 'Twill be hazardous to poison him more!"

"Calm thyself – thou wilt show the world our intent if thou art so lily livered!" Brother Andrew continued unruffled.

His cruelty made him bold and his brothers feared him. He took control and instructed them.

"Wilfrid, 'tis thy task now… thou canst serve the abbot's breakfast as ye do each day, 'twould be no hardship for thee to season his porridge and wine."

Wifrid smirked slyly, nodding in malevolent agreement.

The following morning the malicious monk concealed a small glass vial beneath his scapular. He went to the abbot's kitchen to take the gruel to him. As he scooped the porridge into the wooden bowl he uncorked the vial and tipped half the liquid into the mixture. He stirred it carefully and placed a cloth over the bowl to carry it to the old man. Wifrid carried the food to the chamber where the abbot lay. He rested the bowl on top of the cupboard, while he poured wine into a cup, this time emptying the last drops of the potion into it. He mixed both wine and porridge well with sweet honey to mask the bitter taste. The abbot ate and drank heartily after his purging the day before and rested on his bed. The poison soon spread silently through the old man's system, withering his life force as surely as if he had been bitten by a serpent. He grew pale, his skin growing waxy and grey. He lost his senses, shivering uncontrollably, his whole body wracked with violent convulsions until he lay finally still and at peace.

Wilfrid did not betray his guilt, feigning shock and grief when the abbot was proclaimed dead. His salty insincere tears flowed freely down his cheeks, his eyes seeming to sting with deceit. The infirmarian, unsuspecting of foul play, had been unable to provide an antidote and his possets were useless against the toxin. He blamed himself for his lack of skill and care of the old abbot.

The murderers were confident that their crime would not be revealed and were sure they had left no clues to incriminate them. The abbey was in mourning and a vigil was held for the abbot in the church. All was secure. The three hung their heads in false sorrow, each one silently acknowledging their part in the poor abbot's demise.

As the quire monks prayed for the soul of abbot Laurence an eerie silence fell upon the church. An inky shadow stained the nave, palled in a midnight shroud. The monks froze and fear struck their hearts as the unnatural darkness surrounded them. A pinpoint of light appeared behind the funeral bier. The strange light grew and glistened. Its incandescence came from within the aumbry in the presbytery. Contained within the cupboard was the chalice, which had held the fatal sacrament. The silver chalice shimmered like a guiding star, summoning the brethren to see its strange ethereal radiance. It proclaimed its innocent part in the murder of a saintly man. A holy vessel tarnished by this evil deed, now transformed into something sacred…

Ye evil brothers were terribly disturbed by the strange revelation and after Vespers, slipped silently into the night, never to be seen again, but condemning themselves as surely as if they had confessed. A hue and cry was set up to catch the miscreants, but to no avail. A jury declared these monks were responsible for the death of Abbot Laurens and condemned them to not rest until penance had been done. The superstitious peasants tell tales to this day that their spirits are trapped, unable to leave the abbey precinct until their sin is spent. The chalice became an abbey treasure, as prized as those other sacred objects housed within. Safe in the sacred walls of Furness Abbey for an eternity…

Pray for us ye Blessed Abbot Laurens

Chapter 8

Back home again

"So that is the special treasure which we are tasked with protecting," concluded James solemnly.

"Well, what are we supposed to do? I don't know where it is, do you?" asked Rob.

"No, but we will have help to find it I'm sure… the old monk will help us. It disappeared at the time of Henry VIII when he destroyed the abbey" James grinned. "He didn't do such a good job; it would have made my job much easier had he got rid of it more completely. You have to look in your world and I in mine. It cannot be too difficult."

"If you say so!" said Rob, unconvinced.

"Well, I think it is time for us to return you to whence you came!" said James standing up straight.

"How do you know it's time for me to go?"

James grinned from ear to ear and nodded towards the door. A spectral figure hovered, transparent but visible; the monk was indicating that they should return.

Rob shuddered.

"He still creeps me out, however good he is meant to be."

They returned at a steady rate of knots back to the abbey.

"When will I see you again?" he asked.

"In time, in time…" James said soothingly. "We will be reunited, for it is our fate to reveal this treasure."

They walked in silence towards the tunnel. The light was fading and a solitary hoot of an owl echoed across the empty abbey. With the briefest of goodbyes, they shook hands firmly and Rob disappeared into the darkening mouth of the tunnel. Rob scuttled crab like along the uneven tunnel and emerged at the other end. Here it was dusk too, but he could hear the hum of traffic and could see the streetlights around the edge of the abbey. He was locked in of course, which was a nuisance, but he soon climbed over the railings into the road and began his walk home. He shivered and his mind was flooded with the memories of the last hours. A sudden movement from the trees in Abbot's Wood startled him and a lustrous black raven flew low, almost clipping his head.

He panicked and began to run. The raven flew above him and cawed as if to warn him. At the end of the road, where it forked, a sleek black car stood, its lights dipped, waiting silently for him to pass, like a lion stalking his prey. Rob glanced at the raven and whispered a silent thank you. He climbed swiftly over the fence and sped down into the field to make good his escape. He ran unseen into the lane and sprinted as fast as he could until he reached home… and safety.

As he lay in his bed mulling over the events of the day he began to wonder if he had dreamed the whole episode. He considered the places that such a treasure would be concealed. It could not be in the abbey itself or it would surely have been discovered. Where could it be? Who knew? He toyed with the idea of talking to Nate about it but decided against it. He didn't want him to think he was completely mad. He would wait until things unfolded a little bit and then tell him. He knew this must have something to do with what his brother and sister were involved in but it seemed clear to him that his task was a different and separate one.

True to journalistic form Rob began researching James Ramsden the next morning. He had heard of him but didn't know much about him. He was fascinated with what he read… the stories of his exploits were easy to find on the Internet and in his mum's collection of local history books. He had been quite a guy! Apparently, he had overseen the development of Barrow in its early days and had created a large bustling town from nothing. He had never thought of Barrow as an important town – he always thought it was a bit dull and not a place of opportunity. However, it had been in James' day, some bright spark had coined the phrase, 'the Chicago of the North' to describe it. Who would have thought it?

He was amazed to find that he had a mansion up in the woods above the abbey. He had not known that Abbot's Wood was the estate that James Ramsden enjoyed in his life time as a reward for his service for Furness Railway.

He chewed on the end of his pencil and mulled over the things he had read. Maybe it would be a start to have a look around up there. He didn't expect to find anything but there had to be a reason for his meeting with James, so it made sense to explore where he had lived. He smirked when he thought about the tiny cottage he had been taken to and wondered how long James had had to wait to get his dream house.

He drove to the abbey that afternoon and parked at the amphitheatre. Rob walked up the hill and up the steps into the wood. It was fairly deserted apart from a couple of dog walkers. The late summer sun was warm and he was sweating by the time he reached the top. He followed the path towards the site of the house and instinctively kept looking behind him. Nobody was there. A couple of magpies were perched in the trees, but he hardly noticed them. As he neared his target the birds flew swiftly down to the abbey, silently gliding into the sandstone remnants.

Rob stopped at the massive sandstone blocks, which surrounded a flat grassy lawn. They were the last surviving relics of what must have been a magnificent building. The blocks were arranged in two lines forming half of the rectangle. A sign explained that then house had been damaged by fire and that it was then demolished by the council, to make a nuclear bunker. Rob raised his eyebrows, wondering who the lucky occupants of the bunker would have been if war had broken out. The sepia picture showing the house made him speculate about who decided it would be a good idea to destroy such a lovely building.

He leaned against the stones and thought over the

recent events and the warm rays of the diminishing summer sun made him drowsy. He yawned widely and closed his eyes for a moment. When he opened them he found someone standing in front of him, blocking out the sun. He jumped with surprise, it was that strange kid again… the last person he had expected to see.

The boy peered at him and grinned.

"Dozing off then were you?" he said.

"What do you think?" retorted Rob, returning the grin.

"Well, come on then, I have to show you something!"

Obediently Rob stood up followed the boy… but stopped almost as soon as he had begun.

The world was spinning and everything blurred reminding him of when you went on a fairground ride. He was disorientated for a second or two and then he steadied again. The momentary relief was soon overcome by a huge wave of panic. The world around him had changed. The stones he leant on were there no longer, or rather, they were but arranged differently… very differently indeed. Before him was an amazing building, built from the very stones he had rested amongst. It looked dilapidated; true – but it was still incredible. A gothic mansion rose from the overgrown and unkempt gardens, still impressive but uncared for. Men were working in the distance and hammering and banging echoed across the garden.

"James lived here you know!" Titch said abruptly.

Rob stared at him.

"Really? You know him too?"

"Course I do – I know lots of things that you don't know yet!" he chuckled, "And I deliver meat up here for the big house. Course that was before the old man died and it all went to rack and ruin… shame it was a lovely house."

"The old man… James?"

The boy shook his head.

"Nah… Fred his son… only had the one and *he* never married,"

Rob took a moment to reflect upon this information.

"Ok, so why are we here… *Titch*?" he winced as he said the name.

"You don't get it do you? We're all involved, we have to save the abbey treasure and James is part of it too."

Without further ado Titch scrambled through a hedge and across the remnants of a formal rose garden. It was tangled and overgrown, the roses had turned wild and had become briars, which caught and tugged at their clothes as they pushed their way towards the house. As they neared the door they noticed two builders carrying a ladder into the other end of the house. They crept in and tiptoed into the hallway. The house was empty and the only evidence of recent occupancy was paper strewn across the floor, odd items here and there which looked as though they had been dropped or left behind by someone moving out in a hurry. They skulked along the passage to a huge wooden door with a brass plate and handle. Titch pushed the door ajar and they could hear the two men further along. They crept into the dusty room and next to the window was a battered screen – once an elegant and essential addition to the house – and some tea chests. They scuttled behind the screen and hid quietly. Rob felt quite conspicuous being much taller than the boy, and crouched down as low as he could.

The two men came noisily into the room. They laid down their jackets to sit on and took out tins holding their sandwiches and a thermos flask of tea. The younger man was talking to his companion and instead of sitting and wandered around the room.

"Hey Ted, it was quite a house this wasn't it?" He whistled as if to emphasise his point.

"Aye, it was."

"They must've been rich them as lived 'ere too! All these rooms… and not to mention the garden."

"Aye, they must," agreed Ted.

"I'd have like to 'ave seen it… y'know in its heyday! Must've been summat posh!"

"Aye, that it was," Ted nodded.

The young man bent to look in the massive chimney place. As he stood he banged his head on the over mantle. He looked at the considerable shelf and decided it was a better option than sitting on the floor. He managed to find himself a comfortable spot on the low mantle, legs dangling and leaning back against an ornate mirror behind him. He shoved the remainder of his sandwich into his mouth and turned to look at the mirror. He stroked the fancy frame and ran a rough hand along the base. He shouted in surprise as he caught his finger on a small metal catch at the bottom. As he put the grazed finger in his mouth a remarkable thing happened.

Behind him the mirror shot upwards revealing a secret room stacked with an amazing array of artefacts. The two boys concealed behind the screen could hardly contain themselves. The same thought flew through both of their minds. What if the treasure was concealed in there?

"Cor Blimey Ted! 'ave a bloomin' look at this lot!"

The taciturn Ted was even more uncommunicative than usual! His mouth dropped open and he jumped to his feet quickly to see what lay behind the mirror. It was an Aladdin's cave full of valuable and beautiful objects. Why the items were concealed there was hard to say, but someone had gone to great lengths to safeguard the booty. Silver vases and ornaments glinted in the dim light, carvings and statues created curious shapes in the gloom and on a piece of furniture lay a wad of papers, sprinkled with a layer of dust, undisturbed for years.

"Right lad!" said Ted, "we'd best go 'n tell gaffer… they can't know about all this! Pick yer stuff up and we'll get movin'."

The young man opened his mouth to protest but Ted was having none of it. He propelled him from the room and closed the door with a bang.

The boys came out of their hiding place and raced to the gaping opening over the fireplace. Titch climbed nimbly onto the shelf and disappeared inside.

"What can you see?" cried Rob.

"Come and see for yourself… hurry up they might be back soon!"

Rob obeyed and found himself amongst a collection of items that looked as though they had come from a museum.

"Do you think the chalice is here?"

"I dunno… just look…we must be meant to find something."

The boys examined the items closely – hoping that amongst the candelabra and urns there would be a silver goblet, but to no avail. They found all manner of exciting things, not least a white sailing cap, which must have belonged to someone with maritime interests.

"Hey! Look at this…" Rob's voice trailed off as he read a long document from on top of the small bureau.

"It says…the last will and testament of…"

"Who? Whose is it?"

"James Ramsden, Knight of the Realm…"

"Aw no…" dismay washed across Titch's face.

"Well, it doesn't say anything about the treasure from what I can see."

He rustled the other papers and as he dismissed each one in turn, he discarded them onto the floor beside the bureau.

Suddenly, he froze. The hairs prickled on the back of his neck as he read the front of a yellowed envelope, stamped with the distinctive crest of a Rams head… for Ramsden.

The name on the front was his, written in Victorian schoolboy copperplate handwriting.

Before he could open it a noise drifted in from the gardens. The men with "the gaffer" were on their way back. The boys jumped down from the mantle and ran to the door they had come through. Just in time they escaped into the hall and out of the door to the gardens. They ran and ran until they were hidden by the trees and bushes. Sweating, red-faced, scratched and torn they sank onto the long grass and caught their breath.

Rob was still clutching the envelope and he gazed at it incredulously.

"Well open it then!"

"Give us a minute…"

He carefully peeled open the envelope moving the wax seal gingerly so as not to damage it. He smiled as he could just make out a small replica of Abbot's Wood house itself on the wax.

He slipped out the piece of paper and slowly unfolded it.

Abbot's Wood,
Barrow-in-Furness
Lancashire
5th August 1896
Dear Rob,
It is some years since we met and we have unfinished business to

complete. When last I spoke with you the chalice which Brother John entrusted us to seek was in peril of discovery by those who would do ill. It was hidden by me and I have waited long to reveal its location to you, but you did not come.

I despair of you ever finding it because you have so long been gone and I now am an old man and not in great health. I would have liked to pass this task to my only son Frederic, but am not yet sure he has the mettle to do it. I tried many times to find you at the places we met before and the brother too has not been visible to me for some years now.

It is with heavy heart that I leave this letter for you with the one hope that it will avail you of the help you need to find where it is hidden.

In the interest of safety I have left you one clue here and you must follow the others to reach what you seek.

God speed and I pray we will meet once more, but I am weakening now and I believe my time cannot be long.

Your obedient servant

James Ramsden

Look...
Where first I surveyed Barrow Town,
Upon Rabbit Hill
My image and my name preserved in stone
A sign to see
Of clean white purity
Shining bright in summer light
Follow its image to a hallowed chamber beneath
Cuthbert's emblem will guide thee

CHAPTER 9

A SURPRISE

They fell silent after reading the letter. Both boys felt sad because they believed that they would probably not meet again in this life. It seemed strange to be mourning a man who was actually dead before either of them had been born. They lay back in the grass contemplating the strange afternoon they had spent. They chatted about all kinds of things, including family. The more the boy said the more Rob became convinced that he was indeed Granddad's younger self. This was confirmed when he invited him to use his given name… George. Rob accepted this information but his inner disbelief still confused him.

When George sat up he caught his breath. The house and gardens shimmered like a mirage in hot weather.

They were no longer in an unkempt overgrown garden. It was splendidly laid out, filled with beautiful flowers and exotic plants, carefully laid paths ran back and forth and the house rose splendidly behind it. A long drive wound its way through the tree-lined wood to the grand house.

George pummelled Rob in the shoulder to attract his

attention. Rob looked round in amazement. The boys stood up and ventured nearer to the house, which was resplendent.

Suddenly, from behind the hedge an elderly man walked into the rose garden. He stopped dead in his tracks. The boys stopped too. The recognition was instantaneous.

It was James. A much older James than the one they had seen before. He was bald and his face was fringed with greying sideburns. He was distinguished, dressed in a smart suit and walked with a silver topped walking cane. He beamed at them and something of his youthful self was revealed.

"I have long awaited this meeting. It has been too long, though I see you have not aged a day!"

He marched purposefully towards them.

"We have just…" began Rob.

"… been wondering when we would see you again!" interrupted Titch.

He scowled and shook his head to prevent Rob from saying more about what they had discovered.

"How goes the quest? I have seen nought of the monk and am at a loss to know where to look, though I do have some ideas."

"Well, James we have been lost too… we need some help, there are no clues," Titch looked hopefully at him.

"Then come with me for I may have found something which might help somewhat."

James strode off towards the remarkable house.

The two boys followed him, wondering what it

could be that he had found. They found themselves in the same drawing room they had been in earlier, but this time it was furnished, packed from floor to ceiling with items, which they would regard as museum pieces in their days. James beckoned them to sit down in the armchairs and he then left the room momentarily.

"What did you say we didn't know anything for?" hissed Rob, "We've got his letter!"

"We can't tell him we've got it because he might not write it and leave us the clue… he hasn't found the chalice yet or he would have said."

Rob saw the sense of this and was glad he hadn't blurted out the news. James returned and sat opposite them clutching a heap of papers and maps.

He sighed and smiled at them. His eyes twinkled youthfully.

"Welcome to my home," he said proudly. "I have come far since I last saw you."

Rob grinned, "You have indeed. What are you now… mayor?" he laughed.

James smiled.

"It is strange you should say it but this honour has been bestowed upon me only recently. In fact I have even been made a knight of the realm this very year. "

Rob grinned.

"They'll be putting a statue up for you next!" he chuckled, knowing that this is exactly what would happen.

James sat down and unrolled the maps, anchoring them with heavy paperweights. He traced his finger along the parchment as though he was following some invisible route.

"Look!" he beckoned to them to come closer.

They bent over the table and forgot that James was now old enough to be their father. The boyish excitement chased away the years and soon the three of them were absorbed in examining the old map.

"You see… this is an old tithe map, showing many places which we no longer see. I have looked at these papers for clues many times. We used them to discover where old water courses were and mine workings from the old days, when we were planning the new route of the railway."

"What did you find? Anything useful?" asked Rob.

"I believe I did," he replied.

He grinned and leaned closer into the map, taking out a pair of spectacles and peering through them. He stabbed at the map with his forefinger.

"Here!" he said, "What do you see?"

The two boys peered closely at the place he was indicating. Both took a breath and stepped back.

"You see! You think it is a clue too, don't you?"

Rob grinned and nodded.

Just as they were about to discuss the find the door opened and an impressive lady swept in, her long skirts rustling as she walked.

"James," she sighed, shaking her head, "I thought you were taking a break from your work? You need to rest as the doctor instructed."

She looked at the two boys as though it was the first time she had seen such creatures.

"And who, pray, are these young men?"

"Er… they are two young engineers who wished to see some of the old plans… I will rest when they leave, my dear, I promise." James looked sheepish.

"Well, see that you do. I will ask the maid to bring some tea and scones for you all."

With that she left the room.

"That was close," said Titch.

"It was. I would not wish Hannah to know of my quest. She fusses so."

"What's up with you then?" asked Rob bluntly.

James sighed and shook his head.

"I have a malady which tires me sorely and has no cure. My doctor insists I reduce rich foods and sweet pastries… though I doubt this helps," he added grudgingly.

Rob raised his eyebrows. He wondered what illness it was and decided he would Google it later.

"No matter," James brushed away the thought.

They returned to the old map.

"You see," he said, stabbing at the map with his index finger, "This must mean something."

He indicated a blot on the map of the valley. The boys both peered closer to see what he was excited about.

The map showed the winding river which meandered through the abbey and out to sea through the low-lying salt flats. It passed through a small group of buildings, which were marked as Park House Farm.

"Can you see… here?" he stabbed at the paper again. "It was an abbey grange…"

"What's a grange?" asked Rob.

"It was farm belonging to the monks… they had tenants or lay brothers working them… and some of this is as old as the abbey and some of it was rebuilt after the dissolution with stones from the ruined abbey."

"Ok… but why do you think it's there? How do you know?" interrupted Rob.

"It would be lost at the time of the abbey's destruction. The monks concealed the most important treasures when the King's officers came to ransack the abbey. What better place than somewhere close by, but a place the monks had easy access too? But more than that – can you see the symbol drawn beside it?"

The boys leaned in again and tried to decipher the crude drawing. A distinctive image of a goblet adorned with leaves and berries jumped from the page.

"It looks like the chalice… and …"

"Deadly nightshade, just as in the story," added James.

He rustled the other maps and pulled out two more which looked older than the first. One was on parchment and was a very primitive plan of fields and buildings.

"Look at this one, from the time before the abbey was destroyed. The grange is still there, with fewer buildings but there is no similar mark. But then later, this one, which is dated 1547… when the land had been parcelled up and sold. It has a mark which I believe to be the cup."

There, inscribed in the body of the farm building

was a simple picture of a U with a short line dissecting it through the middle. It was not as obvious as the first and had no leaves or berries, but it did appear to be a cup.

"Wow! Have you been to look then?" demanded Rob.

"As I said I have been unwell. However, I am *much* better now!"

James grinned, the years melting away as he regained his youthful spirit of adventure.

The three of them looked knowingly at each other and set off towards the door, only to meet with the maid, bringing the refreshments, which Lady Ramsden had arranged. After she had gone they made a perfunctory attempt to eat and drink. None of them felt hungry and hurried to start their next task. They crept out as quickly as they could, avoiding being spotted by Lady Ramsden. James seized the maps as he left. They walked quickly through the gardens, down the drive and past the gatehouse, which was much smaller than in Rob's time. A lady was just entering the house and she was taken aback to see James. She smiled and bobbed a curtsey in deference to Sir James, as she knew him.

He in turn doffed his hat and walked speedily on.

"Keep walking it's my butler's wife!" he hissed, "She will be curious to see me walking this path by foot… I usually take the trap."

They walked along the small lane and slowed their

pace. James was sweating and his florid face told them that he rarely took exercise. They walked into Park House farm over a simple footbridge, across the railway line. The farm looked rustic and primitive, with none of the farmyard machinery of their centuries. Farm hands were working in the barns and paid no heed to their illustrious visitor and his companions. They walked around peering at the buildings, looking for some indication of where the chalice might be hidden.

They arrived at the courtyard where the main farmhouse stood and rested against a wall. James ran his handkerchief beneath the water pump and wiped his face with the cool water. His hand stopped abruptly, giving him the look of a statue frozen in time. He was staring at the lintel above the dairy at the side of the house. Carved into the sandstone was a delicate sprig of leaves and berries, set in a circle.

"It's the nightshade!" cried George.

"It most certainly is!" agreed James. "And I'll wager the circle binding it represents the cup."

They collectively rushed towards the doorway almost knocking a young woman over. She wore the dress of a dairymaid and her fair hair escaped in wisps from beneath the cotton cap she wore. She steadied herself and looked directly at them. Her eyes widened when she realised who the older gentleman was. She had seen him before, driving past the farm in his carriage with his lady wife. She dropped a quick curtsey, but Rob wasn't quite so sure she really meant it. There was something slightly rebellious behind those brown eyes. He smirked to himself; maybe she would end up becoming a suffragette?

She placed her hands on her waist and stood her ground blocking their way.

"Can I help you Sir?" she asked.

James was taken aback and raised himself to his fullest height, affronted by the apparent challenge.

She stared back defiantly.

"I am Sir James Ramsden, Mayor and Director of the Furness Railway Company and who might you be?" he answered indignantly.

"My name is Leonora, Sir, Leonora Sheriff. My friends call me Lee and I work here in the dairy."

"Well, Miss Sheriff, I would be grateful if you would stand aside and permit us entry!"

The young woman narrowed her eyes as she observed James closely. For a moment he wavered, thinking she was not going to allow them to pass. However, he had piqued her interest and she stepped aside, smoothing down her apron.

James strode past her opening the heavy wooden door. The boys followed but Lee marched in straight behind them. She grinned at them, her nut-brown eyes crinkling with amusement. Whatever mystery they were hiding she was not going to be left out. She closed the door firmly behind them. James raised his eyebrows and his mouth set in a disgruntled scowl. Rob and George looked at each other; they had not seen this side of his character before.

James looked imperiously at her and he had obviously decided that he couldn't get rid of her for the moment. He used his politician's skills to turn the situation to his advantage.

"Have you seen anything… strange in here?"

"Er… think you might have to be a bit more specific James!" suggested Rob.

He shrugged and relaxed a little, some of the pomposity escaping like air from a balloon.

"My dear, have you seen any images like this one?" He indicated the picture on the plan he had brought from the house. She gazed at the plan closely scrutinizing it.

"I have not seen the goblet, but there are sprigs of nightshade all around this building," she pointed at the drawing of the plant.

James and the two boys could not contain their excitement.

"Show us please!" demanded James more politely than before.

Lee nodded and led them to a small passage to another part of the dairy. There on the flagstone was the perfectly executed carving of a nightshade plant.

"Here" she said unnecessarily and continued walking.

They followed her to the scullery through an arched doorway. Again on another flagstone was the remnant of a carving, worn with the constant traffic of feet over the years, but still recognisable.

"And here…" she moved to another smaller room, indicating the carving on the lintel as she passed through.

"And here!" she rested at a walled well, covered with a wooden lid. There around the rim were four more.

"Is that it… there are no more?" asked James.

"No Sir, this is where they end. What does it mean, if I can be so bold?"

The three conspirators shot a fleeting glance to each other. They gave silent approval to James and he revealed their quest simply to her.

"So there is treasure here? But where? There is only this old well, you can see the bottom and there's nought there!" she looked doubtful.

With that the boys lifted the lid and removed it from the head of the well. The four of them leaned over the low wall simultaneously to see if the treasure would reveal itself. George felt around the inside edge to see if there were any marks or clues. None were apparent. He leaned so far over that he almost fell in. The obvious solution was to use the rope and bucket to travel down the shaft. It wasn't too deep and seemed easily accessible. George prepared to clamber on top of the bucket to be lowered down. It was a good job he was so thin and light as the bucket was not large. James and Rob helped him to grip onto the rope and began to wind the rope down slowly. George felt around the walls as he went further down, checking for protrusions and bumps. He was just above the shallow water and had almost given up when he jerked the rope for them to stop.

"There's something just above the water line. It looks like sacking or something," he cried.

In their excitement they released the gear and the rope drop down suddenly. The sudden movement jolted George and he slipped from his perch into the cold water.

"Argh! It's freezing!"

He was up to his chest in water. At least now he could examine the find more easily. He waded to the side where he had caught sight of it. He tussled with the sack pulling it until it came loose. With it came a brick, falling heavily with a splash into the water. The hole that was exposed was dark and dank and had evidently not been open to the air for many a year. George reluctantly put his hand into the grimy aperture. It felt empty apart from soil and mould. He pulled it out and shook his hand to remove some of the dirt.

"What ya doin'?" called Rob.

"Huh! I'm having a tea party! What do ya think I'm doing?"

He rolled up his sleeve and shoved his hand back in the hole, cringing as he did so.

He pushed his hand right to the back this time and felt around in the dark. He caught his hand on something hard and metal. He yelled out to the others.

"I've got summat!"

The three at the top leaned further over the well looking down, where they could see a small silhouette moving in the water below.

He grabbed the object and tried to bring it out but it wouldn't budge. After minutes of scrabbling about, the object moved back, disappearing into the back of the wall. A grinding noise arose from the base of the well and the water level began to drop and flow through a small culvert, which had been revealed. A sluice gate had lifted and the water drained out. Within seconds George was standing in mud, soaking wet and cold. He shivered, more through cold than anticipation. As he knelt to look beneath the culvert he espied a small fall of bricks further along the tunnel.

"Are you safe young lad?" cried Lee. She was beginning to regret allowing them access to this well.

There was no reply. George had scrambled into the small tunnel to where the pile of bricks lay. They were covered with clay and slime and the whole place smelt damp and unpleasant. He picked through them gingerly until he reached the base of the tunnel. Nothing! He could hear the others above, but he moved further on. It was very dark and he could hear gushing water somewhere along the water system. The tunnel dropped in height and he banged his head on a block of stone. He rubbed his head and instinctively put his hand above to feel what had hit him. The stone was smooth with the constant passage of water over years, except… for a carving. He didn't need to see it to know what it was. His heart skipped a beat and he pushed the brick. It gradually moved and slid to one side. At the same time something fell from the gap above and hit him on the forehead with a clunk. As he retrieved it from the mud, he knew exactly what it was. Before he had the time to enjoy his triumph he heard a rushing noise ahead of him. He panicked momentarily as he realised that the water was rising and gurgling around his feet. The culvert was filling up again. He scrambled to the exit as fast as he could, clutching the prize tightly. He fell into the well and grabbed onto the bucket, calling to them to haul him up instantly. James, Rob and Lee mustered all their strength and wound up the rope as fast as they could. Water splashed around the interior of the well and as they lifted a bedraggled boy over the wall the level had risen to half way up the shaft. Had George not managed to get out as quickly as he did the end could have been very different.

Breathless and tired he released the object from his clutch and it rolled onto the slate floor. The clink of metal was unmistakeable and it came to a halt at Rob's feet. It was heavily tarnished, but the bejewelled chalice must have been spectacular in its day. Everyone stood transfixed. James' blue eyes glistened with unspilt tears. They had found it at last!

The two boys were elated and jumped around with happiness. They thumped each other on the back and even James laughed a deep rich laugh. He turned to Lee who was as pleased as they to discover something so amazing. He took her hands in his and peered into her eyes, she was not much shorter than James, being fairly tall for a lady of her time.

"You have done us and the abbey a great service Miss Sheriff. I will not forget this quickly, thank you so much."

He turned to the boys and picked up the chalice.

"You will need to make haste. This must be removed

to your time and place… it is what you came for after all…"

"Ha! Well, I think we've changed history!" said Rob, "You said in a…"

The words were strangled and James never heard them. A gusting wind embraced them and Rob and George were separated from both James and Lee, who stood fixed to the spot. The vortex of energy grew and the images of the two Victorians faded, James still clutching the chalice, and then they disappeared.

The boys grew giddy and spun uncontrollably round and round. When they thought they could bear it no longer they suddenly found themselves back on the grass at Abbot's Wood. The only indication that their adventure had happened was the dreadful state of George's clothes. They were stunned and silent. To have the chalice in their grasp and then to lose it was unbearable. The efforts of the day were wasted and had moved them no nearer to their goal.

They both sat for a time, glumly contemplating the situation.

"So what the heck do we do now?" asked George.

"I haven't a clue-literally!" sighed Rob. "Looks like it's back to the drawing board… we'll have to try and decipher this letter James left us!"

Both boys were near to tears. It was so frustrating and disappointing.

"Do you think we will see him again?"

"I dunno… seems unlikely. He must've written the

letter after we found the chalice," replied George sadly.

So they had not only lost the chalice, but their old friend too. It was too much to bear. This was nearly as bad as when Granddad had died. Rob gulped back a tear, which threatened to escape. That would not be cool. Especially in front of this kid! Rob rubbed the back of his hand across his eyes and down his jeans. He looked over to George. His face looked as sad as he did. He was about to speak when his vision blurred. He rubbed his eyes again and then realised that it wasn't his eyes that were at fault, it was George. He was fuzzy and was disappearing slowly but surely. The lad tried to say something, but Rob could not hear a single word. A sharp pinprick of light was all that was left. Its intensity seared his very heart and he sat staring at the place where his young friend had been for a while.

The dusk was drawing in and he stood up to leave. A sole magpie watched from a tree as he left the woods. A strange cawing echoed through the wood, heralding the departure and was carried through the air, relayed from one magpie to another, monitoring his journey home.

CHAPTER 10

CHRISTMAS IS COMING

Rob had seen nothing of George, the monk or James since the end of the summer. He had been on the verge of telling Nate that he knew there was something going on, but as time went by he dismissed this as a bad idea. He felt foolish and could hardly believe that he hadn't dreamt it. On top of all this the Sixth form was really hard work and he was tied up with essays and other stuff he could really do without. Nate kept himself to himself and even Rebecca seemed a bit cagey… both of them were up to their necks in this strange stuff he was sure. Autumn drifted into early winter without remark and everyone went about their own business, paths crossing but not intruding.

One thing he did notice however, was that every time he left the house a magpie, or sometimes two were perched like sentinels on the tree in the front garden and often he spotted a solitary raven as well. He wasn't a fan of birds and it unnerved him each day when he saw them staring with their nasty beady eyes. They did seem to congregate around their house in large numbers. He had dragged Sam up to Abbot's Wood on numerous occasions to see if there was any hint of the boy or

James, but he was constantly disappointed. Christmas was approaching fast and everyone was busy with plays and events so again there was no time to pin his brother or sister down. He grew despondent and began to think the quest would never be solved. He surely couldn't have dreamt it all could he?

He had been roped into attending Rebecca's concert at Dalton church and was not in a good mood. He sulked all the way up there in the car and grunted when spoken to. He was crammed into an overcrowded pew with the family and he folded his arms disgruntled at being forced to come. The final pressure had been put on by his sister, who reminded him that this was also a service for those who had lost someone recently. She had gone on and on about a star with Granddad's name on it or something – so he had given in and gone.

It had to be admitted, the carols, the candles and the Christmas trees did make you feel a bit warm and festive – but he did it grudgingly. He consoled himself with the thought that at the interval there would be hot chocolate and mince pies. When the break came the congregation milled around trying to reach the refreshments in the vestry. Nate had vanished again and he had seen Rebecca nip off quickly with her friends to get orange juice. He watched her blonde head bob in and out of the crowd and along with her other pals there was one whom he instantly recognised. George was there too. Rob caught his breath and began to push his way through the masses of people. Every step was impeded by somebody getting in the way and he had soon lost sight of them.

He was about to turn and find some hot chocolate when he became unsteady on his feet. He shook his head to clear his brain and ahead of him the colourful lights of the Christmas trees blurred and merged into a rainbow puddle. The light shimmered and grew to an intensity that grew unbearable. Then, with sudden clarity, a new image grew in front of him. The people in the church receded and faded into oblivion as though they had never been there at all.

In front of him a familiar figure was revealed. Sir James was there, older than before, his baldhead shiny, framed with snow white hair, extravagantly long whiskers down each cheek as though compensating for the lack of hair on top. He was smartly dressed in a full topcoat and trousers, with a sleek top hat beneath his arm. He leant heavily upon his silver topped stick and walked ponderously to the window. Rob looked around him, startled. He was no longer in the church; he was in a large grand room with a huge walnut table surrounded by leather chairs. As he moved towards James he glanced around him… the place was familiar. Now he had it! He was in the Town Hall, the *new* town hall – at least in James' time. He called out with a greeting and was excited to see him once again. There was no response.

Behind James was a woman. He took in a sharp breath, the woman was easily recognisable, but she too was much older, with faded fair hair, shot through with silver, tied neatly in a bun and a jaunty hat perched coyly on top. Miss Sheriff was considerably better dressed than when he had previously seen her. However, her spirit shone through and she looked like a woman to be reckoned with. Rob smiled to himself. It looked as though she had risen in status and appeared to have a more important role than a dairymaid now.

The two stood together like conspirators, looking rather conspicuous in this enormous room. James looked wistfully out of the window, onto a wide road bounded by small shops and buildings. Trams made their way sluggishly along Duke Street, which was busier than in modern times. The people bustled about, each on their own mission, oblivious to the dignitary silently observing them from above.

"Well, Miss Sheriff I trust you have made the arrangements?" James sighed heavily and suddenly looked every year of his age. He had shrunk like a withered apple. Rob felt a pang of regret. He was an old man.

"Yes Sir James, I have," replied Lee kindly, patting his arm with a neatly gloved hand.

"Good, good. You have secured the place? My chapel is complete and the hiding place has been constructed?" he asked anxiously.

"I have secured all and it is complete. Please do not distress yourself."

"And the church warden? He is with us? He is of the

Brotherhood?" he continued, ignoring her comforting words.

"He is Sir James you need not worry on that account. Nobody will even suspect the hiding place. It has been masterfully done."

"Good… good. I have the letter ready. I fear I have not long… and Frederic has not proved he has the mettle for such a task. But where to leave the missive I cannot think, where would be a place which our friends would search when I am gone… and when you are gone?"

His watery eyes brimmed with tears and his frustration quivered through his feeble frame. He was a shadow of his younger self and his vulnerability was obvious. He was agitated and was consumed with the worry that the chalice would be discovered by the wrong person.

"I will not rest until I am sure of the cup's security – In this life – or the next!" he said ominously, momentarily demonstrating his old strength and determination.

He wobbled and struggled to keep his feet.

Lee rushed to his aid and dragged a heavy leather backed chair towards him. He sank heavily onto it and leaned forward onto his stick.

"I have but one hope," he muttered, "That the boys will come back before I pass… if that be a vain hope – and I warrant it is, – that they find my note with the help of the old monk's magic…"

Rob longed to cry out and tell him that they had found the note, to put him out of his misery.

Suddenly, James sat up straight backed and alert again.

"I know where to leave it! In my house there is a secret space. Nobody but the architect and I know of this. It is a storage place, but it will be just the solution we require. I have stored some furnishings, which we no longer use there; it would be no effort to add this as well. Fred will never find it…"

His relief was clear and he relaxed in the chair for a second.

"But the chalice…" he glanced at Lee, "It is safe… the swan is marked in clear view?"

She nodded.

"Then I can rest easy. Call my man. I must return to Abbot's Wood. I feel quite done in…"

Lee turned to leave.

Rob moved closer to James. His heart was heavy with sadness. James was so pale and frail, he reminded him of Granddad in his final days. He brushed away an unwanted tear. He so wanted to tell him they had the clue… though he had not the first idea how to solve it yet. He opened his mouth to speak.

James looked up sharply. He stared straight at Rob. James could not see him, Rob was sure.

"James…" he whispered.

"Who's there?"

The old man peered straight at him.

"James… it's ok… we got your letter."

No response.

"James!" he almost shouted.

He could hear the noise from the church in the distance. James was receding slowly. He could see Lee enter with a man dressed in livery in the background.

"See! Miss Sheriff – can you hear… there is someone here?" James stabbed the air with his stick. She glanced at the man and shook her head. It was obvious she believed James was hallucinating.

Under protest the old man was helped to his feet. As they almost carried him towards the door Rob called out again, reaching out a hand.

The old man stopped and turned around.

"We have the note!" cried Rob.

In an instant the old chap's face suffused with colour and his eyes brightened. Their eyes met for a split second with the recognition of friendship. The years dissolved and the young man concealed beneath the outward appearance of an old man shone through. The picture shuddered and began to liquefy and as James disappeared, Rob heard him cry out joyously.

"He has it, Miss Sheriff! He has the note!"

Chapter 11

The message

Rob returned home from the carol service a lot happier than when he had left. He was pleased that he had been able to give James peace of mind. However, he was left with a big problem because he had more fragments of the clue, but still had to discover where on earth to look. He read and reread the note to make sense of it. He forced himself to research everything and anything about James Ramsden. Luckily, his house was packed with local history books, but unfortunately they did not reveal their mysteries to him. He gave in and resorted to a trip to the archives and library.

He spent a few days at the start of the holidays searching records. He located every step of James' life, which was on public record, but was disappointed to find that his diaries had been lost and only fragments remained. He wondered if this had been by design. Who knew what he might have written about?

The chap at the archives was extremely helpful and he made suggestions about which volumes to read and which council meetings to find. He began to put the life story together combining it with his own knowledge of James. He groaned and closed his eyes, resting his head on his hands. He was so tired that he almost fell asleep. When he opened his eyes again a familiar face grinned at him from across the table… or desk as it had now become. Rob glimpsed the surroundings. They were no longer in the modern archives. Instead they were in the old Reference library above. It was an elegant room, battalions of books, journals and periodicals arranged in neat rows, standing to attention. The desks were elaborate affairs, wood and leather and classically styled.

"You struggling?" whispered George.

"Shut up!" retorted Rob.

George chuckled.

The librarian clicked her tongue in disapproval. She was much less friendly than the archivist in Rob's day.

"Well where have *you* been? I've been trying to work this out on my own!"

"Sorry! I have had a lot on you know?" George laughed. "What's happened then? Fill me in!"

"Ssh!" the librarian gestured them to be quiet.

"Come on! Let's go …"

George jumped up and made his way to the door. Rob followed and gazed around him in astonishment. He caught sight of the old museum through glass doors as they ran down the spiral stone staircase. He wondered if this was the forerunner to the Dock Museum in his own time. It looked more intriguing – with stuffed animals and glass cases full of goodness know what! The hi-tech electronic doors downstairs had vanished in preference for an old fashioned revolving door, which creaked as they pushed through.

Rob realised that this slick transit through time was becoming commonplace to him. God knows what time he was in now? It looked early 20th century, but he wasn't sure. As they exited the building he saw the statue of Sir James himself. They both looked across the road, surprisingly lacking traffic, towards the statue. It was a good likeness, but didn't reflect the enthusiasm and sincerity of his personality. He would not have been pleased that his dignity was being contested by a very rude seagull perched on top of his bald head.

He raced after George who was running across the road and along Abbey Road. They dodged in and out of back streets until they arrived at Manchester Street, where George lived. It was a modest street, behind the Co-op bakery and the local newspaper offices. Rob recognised it, but there seemed to be more of it than he remembered, but he knew it might be because some streets had suffered bomb damage in the war. It was a simple street of terraced houses. Children filled the street, playing 'tin can lurky', swinging round a lamppost from a rope or shooting marbles in the gutter. In the distance a man trundled a barrow crying loudly to the householders: "Rag bones, Rag bones! Any owld i'on?" Recycling 1930s style?

They arrived at number 42, with its pristine front step and sparkling windows. The heavy door pushed open easily and revealed a lobby with a carpet runner down the middle, worn and faded, but very clean. They passed a door on the right and George said, "Parlour…

don't go in there 'cept on Sunday and Christmas."

Rob hadn't asked, but was glad he had told him – he wouldn't like to intrude.

They burst into the second room where a cheery fire crackled and burned in the grate. It was homely, with a pair of rocking chairs placed at either side of the hearth. A rug was spread in front of the fire and fire tongs, shovel and scuttle adorned the hearth. On the high wooden mantle there was an array of items, including a pair of quite ugly looking pot dogs that looked as though they should be in an antique shop, a couple of faded photographs in wooden frames and a clock. Above, hung a mirror with a dark wood, carved frame, on a heavy chain; he had seen a mirror like that before… somewhere.

A table covered with a bright white cloth stood at the back of the room and was surrounded by a variety of chairs, none of which matched. A small wooden bookcase housed a higgledy-piggledy selection of books and above it was a small wooden pipe cabinet with a ceramic tobacco jar on top. The one window facing the back yard was draped with net curtains and heavier curtains to the side. The room was bereft of any luxuries and was simply furnished but spotlessly clean and immaculately tidy. Through yet another door was a kitchen with a stone sink, a mangle, a cumbersome cooking range and a dresser laden with pots of myriad styles and colours. Above was a wooden drying rack, draped with an array of shirts and in the centre of the room was another big pine table scrubbed almost white.

At the table a young woman in her thirties stood, kneading bread. She had glossy dark brown hair wound into a bun at the back of her head. Strands of hair fell across her forehead and she drew a floury hand across to push them away. The flour left its mark and George laughed.

"Ha! You've got flour on your face Mam!"

She smiled a beautiful smile, with perfect white teeth, square and even. Her eyes were the same blue as George's and her complexion was one of peaches and cream. She was pleasantly rounded and she looked every bit a mother. Her simple blue dress was covered by a snow-white apron, with thick black stockings and sensible shoes to match. She wiped her hands on her apron and smiled.

"Would you and your friend like a cake and a glass of sass? Your dad brought a couple of bottles… better get some before our Bill snaffles it all," she laughed merrily.

Rob felt as though he had known her for years and warmed to her immediately.

She turned to the oven and took out a huge tray of warm fairy cakes in a greased bun tray. The smell was glorious and she tipped them onto a metal cooling tray. She passed the boys a cake each and George had poured two glasses of 'sass'. The brown concoction reminded Rob of the ginger beer he had sampled at James' home. It tingled on his tongue and was a completely different taste to anything he had previously drunk. The cake was still hot and it melted in the mouth. George's mam continued with her tasks, which not only involved making bread and setting it to rise in a bread mug in front of the fire, but cramming a massive hot pot into the oven to cook for dinner. The cooking smells were appetising and Rob suddenly felt hungry.

The two boys sat in the living room on the rocking chairs. George pulled a small book from the shelf and flicked through it hoping to find a clue to where Rabbit Hill might be. It was a Victorian book, a little foxed and brown but readable. They discussed the note again and Rob told him what he had seen in the Town Hall. They spoke in hushed tones so that George's mother couldn't hear.

"It says about this Rabbit Hill… but I don't know where that is, do you?" whispered Rob.

George shrugged.

He read the note out loud again.

Look…
Where first I surveyed Barrow Town,
Upon Rabbit Hill
My image and my name preserved in stone
A sign to see
Of clean white purity
Shining bright in summer light
Follow its image to a hallowed chamber beneath
Cuthbert's emblem will guide thee

"It has to be a building… 'preserved in stone'… but it could be any building in town."

"We are not going to get anywhere till we find out where Rabbit Hill is…" added Rob.

They fell silent. The book had a map and pictures of Barrow throughout the 1800s they pored over it carefully trying to glean as much information as possible. Suddenly, there it was. On one engraving was a map showing a hill marked Rabbit Hill. It was difficult to make out where exactly it was, but they could see the channel and the piers for loading the iron on to ships.

This located it near to the Strand, one of the main commercial roads in Barrow.

"Mam?"

"Yes George."

"Where is Rabbit Hill?"

"Rabbit Hill? Well it isn't called that now son…"

The boys waited with baited breath for her to finish.

"It's St George's Hill. You know, where the church is?"

Rob punched the air in triumph.

"Thanks Mam…"

"It's a pleasure… why do you want to know?"

"Er… just interested that's all!"

She accepted this simple explanation.

The boys went back to the book and looked for more information. There was another engraving of a church. St George's Church. Beneath the picture was a brief description.

The Church of St George the Martyr was built

during the years 1859–61 by E.G. Paley. Its patrons were the Duke of Buccleuch and Duke of Devonshire; the north aisle was completed in 1867. A later chapel was added in 1883, the patron was Sir James Ramsden. It is known as the Ramsden chapel to this day.

"I think this might be our building!" cried Rob, *"My image and my name preserved in stone!"*

"Come on then! Let's shift!" said George.

Without another moment's delay they left the house.

George's mother called out to them to be careful and on their way out they almost knocked George's dad over. He was smoking a pipe and wore britches to the knee, riding boots and a jacket, well suited to his job as a railway delivery man. He had just returned from stabling his horse. He had on his porter's cap and had a twinkle in his eye.

"Where's the fire lad?"

George laughed and looked at his dad.

"An' who's thee friend? I've not seen him before!" he continued.

"It's Rob, Dad, me new mate!"

"An' where ye goin' in such a rush?"

"Church."

"Church? T'isn't Sunday, hast tha got religion lad?" he said in his strong Cumberland accent.

He chuckled and filled his pipe with tobacco. In seconds a strong aromatic smell filled the hallway and grey smoke wafted around his head. Rob couldn't help but smile. George's dad exuded warmth and friendliness. His face was open and filled with humour.

He thought if he had time to get to know him he would be a right laugh.

They left and ran up the street. Rob looked around still fascinated at the pre-war Barrow. They ran through streets, which did not exist in his time. Where the pedestrianised street and MacDonald's stood in his time there were shops of many shapes and sizes. Dalton Road was a busy vibrant street, shops shaded by awnings, brim full of fresh produce, meat, fish and other goods. The shoppers were smartly or formally dressed and were busy with their tasks for the day – a sharp contrast to the youths in trainers and 'trackies' who loitered about town in Rob's day. It was busier and people milled in and out of the small shops, cyclists rode past, and the odd car trundled its way up the street. They ran on until they reach Church Street.

Rob noticed the pubs, closed in the present, had new life in 1934. As they went past the strange smell of pipe, cigarette smoke and ale mingled and drifted into their nostrils. They arrived at the church, resplendent on the summit of Rabbit Hill. Next to it stood a huge building, North Lonsdale Hospital, endowed by the town elders and dignitaries. As they approached the church they slowed down.

When they walked into the empty church George removed his cap. They talked in hushed tones; it seemed appropriate. Their footsteps echoed as they walked up the central aisle.

"So what are we looking for exactly? And where is the Ramsden chapel?" hissed Rob.

"James image? It said, 'look for my image in stone'. Do you think that he has a statue or summat?"

Rob shrugged. They walked on, looking for a likely clue.

As they approached the steps to the altar, they examined the carvings and even the grand eagle lectern. The stained glass gave no clue and Rob noticed that there were a couple of saints and a swan, but did not recognise anything of significance. They moved towards a small chapel to the right of the altar to explore further. A range of special seats lined the right hand side of the chapel. The Barrow Coat of Arms was above the grandest seat. This was evidently the Ramsden Chapel.

"I think that must be where James sat. This is *his* chapel... the Ramsden Chapel – obvious really," cried George.

"Doh! You could've saved us a lot of time if you'd remembered! I didn't even know he had a chapel, never mind where it was," chuckled Rob.

They walked into the chapel quietly.

The air shimmered like the haze on a summer's day and a myriad of colours shimmered like a rainbow. By now they knew what was about to happen.

The disturbance cleared. A door to the right opened. A tall woman entered. She was dressed in black, for mourning. Her long taffeta dress rustled as she moved. She sported a wide brimmed hat with a veil and a large black feather adorning it. Her dress was tightly structured, pinching in her waist; she presented an elegant figure. She walked past them and knelt at the altar rail.

They watched silently. When she had finished her prayer, she rose and peeled back the veil, revealing a familiar face. It was Miss Sheriff. Granted it was an older Miss Sheriff than they had seen previously, but that determination and purpose still shone through. She looked up at the window as though she was checking something. They edged closer.

She spun around startled.

"Is anyone there?" she cried.

They were standing only a few metres away. She could not see them, but it was as though she could sense their presence.

She turned back to window and then moved to the left. She reached for something with a gloved hand and gently touched it. A grinding noise echoed from the back of the altar. They watched closely but as suddenly as she had appeared she began to disappear. She faded and her image wavered. Finally all that was left was a pinprick of luminescence.

Both boys rushed over to the altar. They looked first at the glass in the window. There was a picture of a swan. The swan was beautifully painted and stood out clearly.

"Look!" cried Rob. "A swan... that *has* to be the symbol of purity that James mentioned in the note. I can't see anything else that would do..."

"I know this! It's St Cuthbert's swan! Your sister has been following the sign of the swan."

"My sister?" Rob exclaimed.

"Yes! You're not the only one on a quest you know!"

"Is it the same quest then?"

"Not exactly, but I told you they are all connected…"

Rob started! "All?"

"Your brother too."

Rob could hardly take it all in. This confirmed his suspicions and provoked many different thoughts about his companion that he could not yet come to terms with. George took charge.

"Come on! We've got to find this!" He scrambled behind the altar rail and inspected where Lee had touched the stones.

Both the boys jumped in astonishment. There he was magnificently carved in stone. A perfect image of Sir James himself, on the opposite side was a companion carving of Hannah his wife.

"Ha! He really did like himself didn't he?" laughed Rob," Having himself carved in the church!"

"Well I suppose that he thought he was important to the town. I expect he thought he had better commemorate himself in case nobody else did," joked George.

"So what was she doing… something moved behind the altar when she touched the carving?"

They felt around and George put his hand over James' face and pressed.

"Sorry James!" he sniggered.

As he pressed the carving it receded into the wall. At the same time gears turned and pulleys moved and the grinding noise they had heard resonated around the chapel. Behind the altar, directly beneath the swan, a slab slid open. The boys hurried to see what it had revealed. A small space had opened and inside it was a roll of soft leather. George carefully lifted it from its resting place. He unwrapped it slowly, revealing a glint of metal. They held their breath in anticipation, hardly daring to believe this was the chalice they had sought. They stood gaping at their prize. It was beautiful, with delicate decoration and studded with precious stones.

"Come on!" We've got to get you… and this back to your time." George said, wrapping the cup again in it leather covering.

Rob nodded in agreement.

As they did so they heard the latch on the door click open. A tall, balding man entered, dark and sinister. His silhouette, framed by the light from the open door made Rob recall the sinister birds he had seen around the abbey. He shivered. George pulled him down quickly. They hid behind the screen on the special pew, reserved for the Mayor and town dignitaries.

"What we gonna do? We can't let *him* get it!" squeaked George.

"He looks familiar."

"Silas Dixon… he is intent on stealing the treasure… "

"I know him! He threatened me and said something about Nate!" Rob scowled for a moment. "So… how is he here? He is from my time… isn't he?"

"He is from any time he wishes to be from. Silas should be guardian of the abbey treasures but has turned to the dark and wishes to possess it for his own ends."

Rob rubbed his eyes with his hand, as if unable to believe this.

Footsteps echoed ominously along the aisle towards the altar.

The boys remained as quiet as a pair of church mice. George shuffled along to the end of the pew and beckoned Rob to do the same. He indicated the door at the other side of the pew. It was the special door the Ramsden's had used to enter the chapel. Somehow, it seemed right that they should make their escape that way. They peered around the doorway to the chapel. The man was engaged at the far side of the church inspecting the walls and the carvings. When George and Rob thought it was safe to move they did with great haste. As they reached the door and lifted the latch, George banged the chalice against the corner of the wall. A muffled clink echoed through the church and the man was disturbed. He looked up and stared at the boys like a wolf observing its prey. The two boys wrenched open the door in panic, slamming it behind them. They leapt down the steps onto the pavement and ran as though their lives depended upon it.

Moments later the man emerged from the church. The chase was in vain; the two boys were swift and agile. George led Rob in and out of back streets until they reached Manchester Street. They were on home territory now and relaxed.

"We can't take this in the house!" said George. "Mam would think I'd pinched it!"

"Well, how do I get it home?"

George looked a bit pale. He was sweating.

"You alright?"

"Nah… feel a bit sick… an' I've got a headache! Probably with all the running."

"You'd better get in then. I'll go back to the library… it seems when I do this time travel stuff I have to go back to where I started. If I don't get back – you'll soon know, because I haven't anywhere else to go."

Rob ran back the way they had come earlier and slipped into the library unseen. He was unsure what to do next to propel himself back to 2005 but decided to walk up the stairs to the reference library. He need not have worried. It was as if the time portal knew he was there. Very soon he was overcome with nausea and giddiness, lights flashing and spinning. He came to an abrupt stand still and closed his eyes to steady himself properly. When he opened them again he was back in the Archives department of Barrow Library. The archivist, a bespectacled gentleman politely shook Rob's shoulder.

"Are you ok, you look a little peaky? We thought you were going to pass out!"

Rob blinked unable to return to reality for a moment. The other younger archivist looked on in concern too.

"I'll fetch a glass of water… that might refresh you," he suggested.

Rob shook himself and his head cleared. It was exhausting all this time travelling.

"Er… no thanks, I feel better now. I'll just go home, I am sure I will be ok now," he answered.

"Well, if you're certain, you need to take it easy. Perhaps you are doing too much studying?"

Rob smiled. He thought how surprised his tutors would be if they heard that.

The two archivists watched him like over attentive nannies, as if they were expecting the worst. He collected his notepad and realised the chalice was balanced on his knee, still wrapped in the leather cloth. He took his coat from the back of the chair and slipped it over the cup – after all you never knew who was watching and waiting to seize the prize.

He retrieved his rucksack from the locker and stuffed everything into it quickly. As he walked through the library he had a feeling he was being watched. He was definitely becoming paranoid. As he left the building the small librarian behind the desk raised her eyes from the cataloguing she was doing on the computer. Her sharp ferret-like eyes had missed nothing. Within an instant she was on the telephone.

"Yes, he has left… no I didn't see anything… but his bag seemed very bulky…" She cackled at the response and replaced the phone into its cradle with a smug self-satisfied smile.

Chapter 12

A race against time

By the time Rob reached his car it had started to snow. The wind was fierce and bad weather was rolling in from the Irish Sea. Billowing dark clouds scudded across the wintry skies and he could not wait to reach home and warmth. He drove along Abbey Road, reflecting how much it had changed from the last time he had travelled along it. He turned into Manor Road and through the West Gate leading to the abbey precinct. The abbey looked powerful and silent, holding its secrets close. It was deserted and night was drawing in fast. As he drove up the hill past Abbot's Wood he noticed a figure by the wall. He slowed slightly in order to drive past safely when suddenly the person stepped straight in front of the car. Rob slammed on his brakes as hard as he could and every nerve in his body stood on end. His heart almost stopped with shock. He fully expected the person to roll across the bonnet of the car.

Nobody was there. He looked around but there was no sign of anyone. Slowly he drew into the side of the road and parked. Rob opened the door and stepped out. He could see no evidence of anyone lying in the road.

"That's just great, I'm hallucinating now," he thought.

He turned around to get back into the car and almost jumped out of his skin. A figure was standing right in front of him. It was the monk. He didn't know whether to be scared or relieved.

The monk smiled. Rob calmed down and looked into the monk's face. He had a kind face and possessed the ability to make one feel tranquil. Rob waited for him to speak.

"My son," he said, "The chalice is in grave danger and thy brother is too. You must find him and his companion once you have hid the cup."

"Nate? Where is he? What danger is he in?" The words came tumbling out.

"Thou must repair to thy home and secure the chalice first. From thence thou wilt take yon iron monster," he indicated the car, "and hasten to thy brother's assistance. The villain Silas is fast approaching the sacred sword and that first must be secured. Thou wilt find them on the road from Rampside. Go now and do my bidding for we have no time to spare."

"What sword? I thought the chalice was the treasure?"

"The sword is not yet secure… 'tis a holy sword and must be saved from Silas just as the chalice must be protected."

Rob nodded. He was brim full of questions but something about the monk's demeanour prevented him from asking more.

"I'll go now…" he ran back to the car.

"God speed my son!" John Stell replied.

The race was on. Rob shot off like a bullet, glancing in the rear view mirror, to take a last glance at John Stell, the abbey scribe. He drove quickly to his house. As he shot into the vacant space next to his mum's car his dad arrived home too. They went into the house together and Rob clutched the rucksack protectively.

"What have you got in there – the crown jewels?" his dad laughed.

"Er… something like that. I'm just dropping it off and I'm going out again… I'll get tea later," he explained.

"Well. You'd better tell your mother. She was already texting me to see where your brother is!"

"Um… I'm going to pick him up we'll be back later…"

He ran upstairs and hid the bag under his bed. Nobody would find it, his room was a tip and they would not be able to see it anyway.

When he was sure it was safe he closed the bedroom door and ran back downstairs.

"I'm going out, be back soon!" he yelled.

He didn't wait for the reply, but as he closed the front door he heard his mum shout a protest.

He leapt into the car and within minutes he was driving along Rampside Road. It was dark and blustery and the rain bounced off the windscreen. He drove slowly so that he could find Nate. The road was empty and very

few cars passed him. Eventually, he saw his brother…
and one of his friends climbing over the fence near the
church; he drew to an abrupt halt.

"Get in! Both of you!" he ordered.

They both gaped at him as if they couldn't believe
he was there. He took charge and although he wasn't
clear about what was happening he knew it was vital to
help these two to solve their quest.

"Where is the sword?" Really? They surely weren't
going to pretend nothing was happening?

Once they were in the car a small amount of banter
passed between them, Rob teasing Tom about his dress
and quaint way of speaking. It really was odd that this
guy felt the need to dress like a highwayman. They were
speeding off towards Aldingham, as he was directed by
the two boys. They drove past the farm and parked
quietly on the edge of the road.

"Where do we go from here then?" asked Rob.

"Into the farm… but we'll have to be careful in case
any of those thugs are about – don't fancy running into
them again!" said Nate.

More words were exchanged and the two boys ran
across the road and slipped down behind the farm. That
was the last Rob saw of them. He went through an
agony of doubt. Perhaps he should have gone with
them, but then that would have meant if anything went
wrong they wouldn't have a driver or someone to alert
the police. Time hung heavily and he had almost given
up hope of seeing them again when they both appeared

from the direction they had left. They jumped into the car and Nate was very agitated. From the rear view mirror Rob could see the headlights of a car in the distance.

"Drive... just drive!" yelled Nate.

Rob needed no further invitation. He put the car into gear and pressed the accelerator down as far as it would go. They raced through the lanes, past Scales and Leece into Stone Dyke and then home.

They had argued about which way to go but had concluded until they had formed a plan; home would be the safest option. They skidded into the drive and hastily discussed the cover story to tell the parents. This involved Tom ridding himself of some of his clothes to make him look more 'normal' as Rob said. As they left the car two malevolent magpies flew so close to them that they almost lost balance.

At the same time a sleek black car purred into the end of the street and parked, turning of its headlights.

"In... now! It's them," ordered Nate.

CHAPTER 13

ENDS AND BEGINNINGS

The following day was the end and the beginning of a remarkable adventure. They had rescued the sacred sword and reunited it with the skull, which Nate had insisted on keeping. All manner of unbelievable events had followed; it had been like an episode of *The X-Files*. Monks, ghosts and all kinds of weird stuff, it was certainly too bizarre for him to cope with.

Rob had watched as his brother said goodbye to Tom, reflecting on the peculiar things that had been happening, not just to him, but to his brother and sister too. What was it all about? Then there was still the chalice to consider – he had to do something with that... you would have thought that old monk might have mentioned it. He shrugged in disbelief. He began to realise that those ideas he had pushed down and ignored were probably all too true. It was all real. After all, he had witnessed monks, long dead, walking the abbey, people from other times; including a fairly famous mayor and not to mention... well he knew now who George really was, even if he didn't quite believe it.

As they walked wearily home along the river towards Bow Bridge a twig flew through the air almost hitting Nate. They looked up and saw George grinning irrepressibly from the other bank. Rob caught his breath and wondered whether to let him in on the secret.

"It's George! It's…" cried Nate.

"I know…" interjected Rob before he could finish, "It's Granddad… like I said it's all been a bit weird recently," he shrugged.

The parting was as emotional as when they had parted once before… that terrible time in the summer when they believed they would see him no more. It was dreamlike and surreal.

"I'll see you again… I promise."

The boy was obscured by the ground mist momentarily and when it cleared there was the old man they knew as Granddad. Behind him was Brother John Stell. He beckoned to George and soon all that remained was an unseasonal white butterfly.

The boys walked home immersed in their thoughts. They caught sight of Rebecca and her friends in the distance. This prompted a conversation and led to more questions than it provided answers.

"Well it all began last summer… do you remember when the garden was trashed?" said Rob.

A solitary black feather fell from the trees, unnoticed. Neither boy spotted the magpies glide silently onto perches along the lane, one by one. Neither did they see the tall figure sullenly surveying them from the distant field. The dark malevolence hung like an oncoming storm in the air. They would pay for this humiliation. He would dig deep into his dark enchantments and draw on his wickedness. They would pay for the banishment of his cousin Ambrose Steele too. They had no right to meddle. This was not their legacy it was his. The chalice must be retrieved; he must acquire the influence it held.

Before the boys had reached home Silas Dixon had formed his plan. Two treasures were already lost to him, but the chalice would be his. He knew it; he could feel its strong spiritual energy drawing him close. It was guiding him like a beacon and showing him its hiding place. He realised those boys had not had time to conceal it properly or to return it to the monk. He still had the chance to gain its power and reveal the greatest prize, which was deeply concealed within the abbey. He had time on his side and would not hesitate to call on those evil spirits who were confined by the abbey's power. He had it within his grasp to change what had gone before and alter time… but he needed the chalice to harness that power.

Chapter 14

A hiding place

Nate and Rob slept right through till mid-morning the next day. They were completely exhausted from their recent adventures. At ten-thirty their sister Rebecca bounced into both rooms, insisting they waken and start the day. She was excited and made so much noise that they began to stir. Nate was up first, curious to discover what she knew of the strange things he and Rob had encountered.

They were talking in hushed tones when Rob came into the living room. He closed the door so that they would not be overheard. The three of them shared their encounters and realised that it was no coincidence that they had been chosen. They were connected by family, both now and in the past, this they understood, but why their family was singled out for this they could not tell. One thing was certain, they could relax a little. The immediate danger was over and all that had to be done was to conceal the chalice safely until they discovered what to do with it.

"The monk must tell us what to do with it," suggested Rob.

"He will appear in time I'm sure," agreed Rebecca, "Do you think we'll see George... I mean Granddad again," she added wistfully.

"I'm not sure... he said he would see us again but... " Nate's words hung in the air.

"We have to find a place to hide the chalice first. Any ideas?" said Rob.

"We could put it where I hid the skull I suppose..." replied Nate.

Rebecca wrinkled her nose at the memory of it.

"Well I can't think of anywhere better. Unless we hide it in the house somewhere?" said Rob.

"Oh yeah, great idea genius! Of course, mum won't find it when she cleans up, will she?"

"Well, if you two boys cleaned your rooms she wouldn't have to," interjected Rebecca.

"Listen who's talking! You're not much tidier than us... she'd never find it in your room, it looks like a jumble sale," retorted Nate.

They fell to bickering and naturally attracted the attention of their mother who was working in the kitchen.

"Will you lot pack it in? For goodness sake, you're like toddlers!" she yelled.

They immediately ceased the hostilities and returned to their discussion.

"So... we hide it in the garden then?" pressed Nate.

"Suppose so... should be safe! We'll have to do it when nobody's around though. At least Silas is out of the picture," said Rob.

"Yes... and Mr Steele has vanished too. So who

exactly are we hiding it from then?" asked Rebecca.

The two boys looked at her closely. What she said was true… but somehow they didn't feel completely at ease. Rob had a squirming sensation in his stomach, as if he was worried about something but didn't know what.

"Well, we don't want to take it for granted. I think we still have to be careful. You know… just in case."

Later that day when the house was empty, Rob slipped into the back garden and lifted the slab beneath the birdbath. He put the chalice, wrapped in its leather cloth, into a cardboard box and placed it in the ground. He covered it over with the earth and replaced the paving stone and the birdbath. He swept away the soil and tidied up. Nobody would ever know anything was underneath the patio. He looked around to check that he wasn't being observed and went back inside to wash his hands. He would tell the other two what he had done later, when they came home. He was pleased with himself and secretly hoped that John Stell would make a quick appearance, take the chalice and then they could get back to normal.

As he went into the house there was a small movement behind the fence next door. An old lady, whom they knew as a kind old soul, had been watching. She smiled and spoke to her little dog quietly. He yapped in response, as if he understood what she had said. A magpie flew up onto the hedge and peered quizzically at her, what passed between them was not spoken, but the magpie understood. He flew swiftly away, over the fields towards the woods to relay his message. A dark brooding cloud passed over the weak winter sun, casting a cold shadow across the garden. Tension crackled in the air and the low hum of unnatural energy seemed to vibrate around the hiding place of the chalice. It was calling out a warning to its protectors, but this time it was in vain, because nobody could hear. The raven appeared and perched on the birdbath, a lone sentry but scant defence against the danger that was coming. Danger; which Rob and the others were unaware of and which would threaten to unpick the very threads of their existence without them even realising.

CHAPTER 15

FOUND AND THEN LOST

That night a storm came. The house was situated on a hill overlooking the valley towards the sea. The wind blew in from the coast bringing with it a bitter chill. Hailstones attacked the windows mercilessly and they bounced against the glass like small bullets. The savage storm was relentless in its assault and the doors and windows rattled noisily, refusing to surrender and allow the wind and rain entry. Rubbish bins were upturned and their contents were blown across the street, tiles slipped and smashed, shards scattering widely and branches groaned and creaked under the pressure. Torrents of rain ran rapidly into full gutters and black puddles bubbled and grew.

Rob couldn't sleep, the howling wind echoed in the chimney and the loft hatch was banging. He was wide-awake, his bed was like a bed of nails and his pillow filled with concrete. He hated being unable to sleep and no amount of rearranging his bed covers and plumping his pillows helped. He sighed heavily and swung his legs out of bed. Everyone else was asleep. He could hear the rhythmic breathing from the next room where his parents slept and a gentle snoring from Nate's room. A sliver of light trickled under the door of his sister's room from her lamp, but when he peeped in she was fast asleep too. He crept downstairs to get a drink to see if that would help him sleep.

The dog was asleep at the bottom of the stairs and he almost tripped over him. Sam grunted and opened an eye to see who had woken him. Rob went into the kitchen and put the hob light on. He took the juice from the fridge and reached to get a glass from the cupboard.

He almost dropped the glass when a shadow passed the window he instinctively drew back behind the wall. The security light at the back of the house was on and strange shadows wafted like wraiths across the kitchen floor. Something.... or someone was outside. Panic flashed through his body like an electric shock.

The chalice! It was in the garden.

The storm was still wild and rain battered the windows. He took a deep breath and looked out of the window. An alarming sight met his eyes. Silas was supervising the removal of the chalice. Other figures were with him, the boy and the woman from his earlier encounter and two of the oddest creatures he had ever seen. Their goblin like appearance made him shudder and he could see red glinting eyes through the rain. One of them spotted him and leapt with incredible agility and superhuman speed onto the kitchen windowsill. Its skeletal hands were flat against the pane and its ugly face was pressed up close, glaring at him. His heart nearly stopped. The creature scratched with a long finger down the glass creating an unbearable noise. He thought the creature would be inside with just a little more effort and he was paralysed with fear. Beyond the animal he could see the others carrying the box and moving away, ready to leave.

Suddenly, Sam awoke, hackles bristling and his lips curling revealing his teeth, bared in a protective growl. He launched himself towards the window shocking Rob into action and jolting the wizened fiend so that it fell backwards onto the patio. Rob unlocked the door, fumbling with the keys. As soon as it was open a blast of wet and icy air splattered him and the dog raced out to attack the intruders. Simultaneously, the rest of the house awoke and Dad rushed in, pulling on his dressing gown. Within minutes everyone was in the kitchen trying to find out what was happening.

The dog had disappeared to the bottom of the garden and there was no sign of anyone else. Dad and the two boys ran outside into the garden, immediately soaked through with the rain. The birdbath was in pieces and a large hole gaped like an open wound. A shovel was abandoned and pots and shrubs had been upturned and dug up. The shed door was swinging open, nearly pulled off its hinges by the wind. The whole garden was a mess. Dad went to close the door and Rob turned to Nate nodding towards the windowsill. Fragments of sandstone littered the sill and the floor beneath, broken splinters and remnants of the goblin were scattered on the paving. Whatever the creature had been, when it fell it had been destroyed.

"Right lets go back inside and get dry," said Dad.

Mum was already handing out warm towels and Rebecca was turning on the kettle.

"I don't know what possesses these kids!" said Dad shaking his head, "Destruction for the sake of it!"

"Vandals! That's what they are. Mindless vandals!" added Mum.

Nate, Ron and Rebecca threw a knowing glance to each other. They knew that it was not vandals who had caused the damage, but they could not tell them who had done it. They would never be believed.

As they drank their hot chocolate and warmed up in front of the fire they all knew that they had lost the precious chalice. The three sat gloomily, minds occupied with ideas of how they would get it back and what Brother John would say about it. A single rumble of thunder growled overhead announcing the terrible loss.

CHAPTER 16

MEA CULPA

A troubled John Stell awoke from his weary and restless sleep. His heart was as heavy as the lead on the church roof. He knew that the chalice was in peril. The crack of thunder heralded the disaster, which he had tried so hard to avert. His eyes prickled with tears. His work was unravelling, time was becoming unstitched… the power that Silas held now could destroy it all and give him the control he wanted and that he, John Stell had thus far denied him.

The echo of the deed reverberated through time, seeping through the walls of the monastery and surrounding all with foreboding. This should have been avoided, he knew. He had tried to place the objects of power out of reach and had assigned through time, guardians to watch over them. He had made mistakes he knew and it seemed to him that all blame rested at his door.

He had safeguarded the book and the sword thus far, but to lose the chalice was devastating as it sealed the security of a much bigger and more important treasure as yet undiscovered and known only to a few of his brethren. He sat on the edge of the straw filled mattress on his wooden palette and looked at his fellow brothers mournfully. They were ignorant to his task, which Abbot William of Dalton had set him those many years since. Only one shared his burden, Robert the Mason. He was a good and stalwart soul however, and John knew he would need to have conference with him on the morrow.

He knew if this was not righted he would not rest, in this life or the next. He knelt heavily next to the bed clasping together his hands in earnest prayer.

"Mea Culpa, Mea Culpa..." he muttered. Panic rose in his chest. His task was undone. He felt it in his old bones. He continued with his prayer... words lingered in the air, hanging like petrified stalactites. His heart was gripped by a cold fist of fear and he despaired of being heard.

His cough returned consuming his weakened body. Suddenly, he fell forward in to the rush strewn floor, struggling for breath.

"Mea Culpa... M..."

Brother Michael awake from his sleep, disturbed by the thud upon the floor.

"Brother John, what ails thee?"

He roused the other sleeping monks and one of the younger brothers ran swiftly down the night stairs, through church and cloister to the infirmary.

Brother John was removed to the infirmary where he was given medicine especially mixed by the infirmarian made from liquorice and comfrey. Brother John fell into a fitful sleep. His friend Robert the Mason was seated beside him as he awoke. The pale face of the monk lit up to see him. He was the only person who now shared his great burden.

"Brother, thou must not worry thyself… this matter will be resolved… thou knowest the boy and his kin are bent on our cause. It can be remedied."

"Nay, Robert! It *must* be remedied… nought can be left to chance."

"'Twill be safe, be assured old friend, thou hast seen those in the future who can stop these evil ones… and they will be frozen betwixt this life and the other for all time, just as those who harmed Abbot Laurence were…" John nodded sagely.

"Aye, but there is a change… I feel it as surely as I take breath… great power is released with the loss of our chalice…"

"We do not know this is so…"

Days passed slowly. Brother John weakened and his cough worsened, Mason watched on helpless, hoping that the prayers said in the Infirmary chapel would heal John's soul and cure his bodily illness. Many days passed with them discussing the safety of the treasures, a feeling of hopelessness washed over them both.

"It all rests with the boy…"

He gasped for breath momentarily.

"He must be certain to pass the knowledge on with care… there must be no mistake. I must remain to help… we must prepare to guide them into the future," his voice rose in panic.

Brother John Stell passed quietly, Robert with him to the end. It was said that his spectre was seen shining brightly in the Infirmary that day. Indeed the story remained potent for years. Those living and working close by the Abbey of Furness told tales of an old monk dressed in white walking the ruins, passing through the trees in Abbot's Wood and along the Precinct Wall, protecting a lost treasure hidden within the abbey walls.

CHAPTER 17

FORGETTING

Rob woke groggily next morning. They had all slept late because of the previous night's events. He had a pounding headache and he felt he had not slept at all. The memory of what they had lost hit him like a sledgehammer. The chalice… it was lost. Rob washed and dressed quickly and rushed downstairs to find the rest of the family having breakfast.

He nodded at Nate and winked at Rebecca in acknowledgement of the secret they held. As he sat down at the table his mum spoke.

"We need to clear up the garden later – can you three help please?"

"Er… yeah…"

"Aw Mum I wanted to go over to Megan's… do I have to?" moaned Rebecca.

Rob kicked her beneath the table. She shot him a look of surprise.

He raised his eyebrows trying to indicate they should see what clues they could find.

She looked blankly at him.

"Go on then," said Mum, "The boys can help."

"Oh great! So we have to do it then?" groaned

Nate. "How come she doesn't have to do it?"

Half an hour later they were in the garden cleaning up again. There was quite a mess and mum had rung the police to tell them about the vandals. The boys looked around for any clues that had been left but they could see nothing unusual except for the heap of sandstone beneath the windowsill where the creature had fallen.

As they cleared the debris away Rebecca and her two friends arrived. They stood around chatting and poking fun at her brothers, which was not received kindly.

"Thought you'd have helped us to find some clues?" said Rob.

"Clues? What are you on about?" asked Rebecca puzzled.

"About the chalice…"

She shrugged and looked confused.

"The what?"

"Have you had a bump on the head or something?" asked Nate.

"I don't know what you're talking about," she replied.

"The treasure! You know! Like the book you found!" he insisted.

"'Course I know about the book – *we* found it after all!" she retorted.

"Well… there was the sword… and the chalice too! You must remember!"

The boys were exasperated.

The girl stared at them. It was apparent that she was sincere.

They did not know what to say. Neither could they understand what had happened to Rebecca's memory. She stood without moving and as they looked at her and her friends they became muted and fuzzy, like an old sepia photograph. It was happening again. The world spun frantically around them and they became disorientated and sick.

They arrived in the middle of a familiar place. They were standing in the Chapter House at the abbey. It was not as they knew it of course. In fact it was spectacular. The boys drank in every detail of their surroundings impressed and fascinated by what they saw. The room was lit with rush lights and candles, bathing everything in a soft orange glow. The walls were painted white, with the bricks pattern picked out in thin red lines. There were delicately carved Corinthian pillars reaching up to the high vaulted ceiling like elegant tree trunks, branching out to support the floor above. The stained glass windows glistened and caught the light like jewels; around the room were carved wooden seats and a lectern in the corner. It was a beautiful place and as magnificent as it was in the 21st century, this incarnation was even better.

Seated ahead of them were two monks, standing beside them was a familiar looking face. Mr Mason, it seemed was there too, dressed in medieval garb, but they were certain it was him. The monk who spoke was by now familiar to them.

John Stell spoke in calm tones, though the concern was etched on his face.

"My sons, welcome. We have much work to do."

They both remained silent.

The other monk, dressed differently to Stell nodded and smiled at them. For the moment he did not speak.

"The task of protecting the abbey treasures was given to me many years past. I have been undone by many misfortunes and grave mistakes and I now find I have put the safety of the abbey and the future at stake by my errors. There are bad influences at large and they now hold power to unravel the good, which is done. Thy sister is already at risk. Her mind has been enchanted by those who would do evil."

The boys glanced quickly at each other, realising that her earlier lapse of memory had been induced.

"This can be reversed if thou canst find the chalice. Thou shalt have help, but thou must move speedily. Those who have been called upon over these many years to assist our cause are locked in time. The boy is the only one who can still pass through. In his time he has had an illness of the mind and is not yet cured. We can use his dream state to bring him through time to aid thee."

"George… do you mean George? He was ok when I saw him… just days ago!"

The three men smiled knowingly.

"Thou canst not rely on thy reckoning of time. 'Tis out of kilter and he is our one hope to rectify this disturbance. We must retrieve that which is lost, for there is yet a greater battle ahead. He fell into illness on the day you saw him last and has caused grave concern to his loved ones. He is strong and will overcome this illness, but it must take its course and 'tis to our advantage to use it. He will find thee and thou must begin thy search before 'tis lost forever."

"Where do we look? An' is Mr Mason gonna help too?" cried Nate, indicating the man beside the monks.

"Nay, my son, this man is not who you think. This is Robert the Mason, his ancestor. But Mason will help as the Masons have always helped."

"The chalice will shine brightly for those who seek it with a good heart. Its power doth wane the further from the abbey it is taken .To gain its fullest influence it must be returned from whence it came. Seek it close by the abbey for they cannot use it well elsewhere."

The other older monk whispered something to John Stell.

"My Lord Abbot says thou must beware of the power they hold and guard thee well because they are not without guile and wickedness. Even for the brief time they hold the chalice they can unravel the threads of time and change that past which we know."

The air shimmered and flickered and the vision of the three people began to fade. The two boys were moving again. When the world stopped moving they were able to breathe properly.

They had returned to their former position, facing the three children in the kitchen. Rebecca laughed.

"You look like you've seen a ghost. What's wrong with you both?"

The boys shook themselves and collected their composure.

"Anyway, we are going out – see ya... wouldn't wanna be ya!" she yelled cheekily as she left through the back door.

"Hmm... not sure I do either," said Nate with a wry smile.

"Know what you mean," replied Rob.

"So... where on earth do we start looking?"

"Beats me... near the abbey I suppose! And Grand... Titch, George I mean... how do we get hold of him?"

Both boys shrugged, still in disbelief that they were friends with their own grandfather in his boyhood. Everything was out of order... out of time even... and none of it made sense. Nate went to the fridge to get the bottle of coke and poured them both a drink. As they drank it they decided to cycle to the abbey again. After all they couldn't lose anything and they needed to have a hunt around to see what could be found to help them.

It was blustery and cold but signs of spring were emerging as they rode into Manor Road and past the farm. Clumps of snowdrops and crocuses broke through the hard earth in the verges and hedgerows and in the field opposite there were some early lambs huddled like little balls of wool next to their mothers. As the boys rode, they past the old Precinct wall stood proud on the ridge above the field and they rode on through the narrow West Gate, in ruins, but still an imposing approach to the magnificence of the abbey. Mill Beck was full and gurgled under the culvert beneath the road into the abbey stream; it was always like this in late winter and often flooded if there was heavy rain. It had worsened since the monk's days because of new houses further up the valley and it was apparent that any further building would seriously threaten the abbey. They splashed through the puddle across the road and rode on to the amphitheatre. They got off the bikes and locked them against the fence.

They walked around the field looking this way and that, unsure of what they were looking for. The abbey appeared harsh and brittle, its red sandstone muted with the dull light, making it dark and forbidding. Grey clouds hung heavily like woollen blankets and everywhere was quiet and muffled. They clambered up the steep sides of the amphitheatre to get a better view from the summit. They reached the top quickly, red faced and panting with their exertion. Resting and taking deep breaths they surveyed the countryside around. It was deserted apart from the sheep dotted about the green fields. As they turned to walk around the rim of the amphitheatre a stick flew unexpectedly from the trees behind them. Both boys looked at each other grinning.

"George!" they cried simultaneously.

There he was hiding in the trees. A wide smile spread across his thin face, eyes twinkling with mirth. His cheeks were ruddy with the cold and his ears stuck out incongruously beneath his navy blue school cap. He had a dark coat and scarf and knee length shorts. His grey socks almost met the shorts but chapped red knees peeped from the gap between the two garments. Rob thought how cold he must be, but the lad seemed not to be aware. His appearance made them both smile.

"So, what do you need me for now? I thought we had finished all of this?" he asked.

"It's the chalice, we lost it!" admitted Rob.

"Lost it? You're having me on!"

Nate shook his head and looked sadly at Rob.

"That is not good!" George commented.

"No, we know that George. Dixon and his lot took it from the hiding place. We couldn't do a thing about it," said Rob.

"What we gonna do then?"

"Er we hoped you might know… the monk said you'd help!"

George grimaced.

"Well… I'll try but I'm a bit fuzzy… I keep having really rotten headaches… should I know where it is?"

The two brothers glanced quickly at each other. This must be the illness John Stell had alluded to.

"We don't know any more than you – except Rebecca is changing…"

"What do you mean?" asked George.

"She's forgotten about the chalice… John Stell said that it was Dixon's conjuring whatever that means," answered Rob.

Nate was wandering into the trees. The others followed close behind.

"This is a funny place," he said.

He glanced around. Sandstone rocks broke through the grass, cracked and uneven. They investigated closely, discovering that the stone had at some time been worked or quarried. There were tools marks on the face of some of the rocks.

"Wow! This must have been where they took some of the stone from to build the Abbey," cried Nate. He clambered over the rocks and began looking closely. The quest forgotten for a moment he knelt to look more closely at something he had discovered.

"Look... it's a carving... I can't believe I have never been up here before... it's amazing!"

The boys looked at what he had found and a strange face leered at them from the rock face, its features ugly and contorted as though in terrible torment. Something about it made Rob shudder. It was evil and reminded him of the gargoyle creatures they had encountered in the night.

"Look! There's another one... and a third!" Nate was astonished at the clarity of the features. One was snarling like a cornered wild animal the lips curled back revealing sharp little teeth, eyes narrowed in a spiteful scowl, the third was even more unnerving. Its visage was one of pure evil, deep grooves and lines driven into the contours of the cheeks, the jaws were frozen in a terrible howl, the sound forever frozen into silence.

A hum of energy crackled through the cold air and their nerve endings tingled. A malevolent atmosphere descended and the glowering clouds seemed to suffocate the sky. The stark trees reached out like black claws threatening and dangerous. Without warning Nate reached to touch the last carving. As he did so a crack of unseasonal thunder rumbled in the distance. The small wood shook and quivered in anticipation. Birds fell silent. George and Rob cried out as he drew nearer to the image. Too late. Their cries were strangled in their throats. His flesh connected with the stone and as it did so a dreadful flash lit up the hillside its pure energy flinging them like rag dolls into the air. They each landed with a thud, the wind forced from them and momentarily stunning them.

When they came to, they were dazed and drained of all energy. Their life force had been devoured leaving them empty. Rob stood up first and reached down, pulling George up by the hand. They turned to Nate. It was clear that he had suffered more than they. He was dazed and his eyes were wild and startled. His unruly hair was standing on end as though he had experienced an electrical shock. He looked at them with confusion.

"Are you ok, bro?" asked Rob, concerned.

"Er… I'm not sure… what happened?" he whispered huskily.

He got to his feet shakily and staggered.

"Whoa! I feel a bit odd… I'm gonna go home Rob!"

"We'll come with you…" he began.

Nate's forehead creased in a frown.

"We? What you on about?"

With that he walked straight past George without acknowledging him. George raised an eyebrow.

"See ya Nate…" George's voice trailed away as it became evident that Nate could no longer see him.

The boy walked away from them and unlocked his bike, riding away without a backwards glance.

"What's that all about? It's like he doesn't know you!"

George shook his head sadly.

"I'm afraid he doesn't. I think you'll find he has forgotten his quest just as Rebecca has. That carving is evil and he has unlocked something lying dormant inside it."

"Oh no! What can we do now? That only leaves you and me to find the chalice. Will they be ok? Can we get them to remember again?" The questions tumbled out.

"How am I supposed to know? I'm only a kid! You're talking like I'm your dad or something!" George shouted.

Rob was startled. Something was happening to George too. He was obviously unaware of his relationship to them… not that Rob had ever been a hundred percent convinced of it anyway.

The young lad looked startled for a moment, his blue eyes round like saucers and brim full of tears. He stared uncomprehending and confused. He tried to speak but the words were jumbled. Rob gulped. This was like Granddad had been when he had the stroke. It couldn't be happening to George at his young age could it? Then he thought about what the old monk had said … *"In his time he has had an illness of the mind and is not yet cured. We can use his dream state to bring him through time to aid thee."* Maybe this was to do with this…

As he looked on in concern the little boy paled and flickered, his young face melting into his older one... Granddad! It was uncanny to see this change in front of his very eyes. The young George returned and faded like an underexposed picture. A snap of white energy and he was gone. Back to square one Rob thought. Nothing could be done now. He had gone. No doubt he would return. He looked ruefully at the stones and the hideous faces. They were somehow to blame for this latest turn of events and he would have to try to lessen he effect. He rode away from the abbey slowly, his legs leaden and heavy. He reached the turning into his road and was relieved to see Nate's bike propped against the garage door. However, his relief was short lived when he went inside the house. Both his siblings were prostrate on the settee, one at each end, white as a pair of hospital sheets and shivering.

They were in a fitful sleep and their skin was as cold and white as alabaster. As the shivering subsided, the stillness of their bodies was eerie – like the carved effigies you found in churchyards or... abbeys. He panicked as he looked at them. What was wrong with them? Fear rose in his throat and he shouted for his mother to come quickly.

She appeared at the door and worry was etched on her face too. She moved towards him and clamped her hand across his brow to check his temperature.

"Are you feeling ok? I've called for the doctor... I think these two have a virus or something."

The words died in his throat. Whatever was wrong

with his brother and sister, it was almost certainly *not* a virus.

This was down to him now. He had to find the chalice. This was the only way to save them from whatever had struck them down so suddenly. George was ill too, in his time –this he knew and who could guess when he would be able to travel back to help? There was only one person he could think of to help… but how would he be able to reach a long dead mayor… and friend? James was the only answer – he would have to summon him up somehow. He did not know where or how, he just knew he had to do it. Before it was too late… before he was out of time!

CHAPTER 18

ALL MIXED UP

The doctor had been and declared that the household was stricken with a 'nasty virus'. Wasn't that what they always said when they didn't know? The two patients were put to bed and Mum was advised to make sure they drank plenty of fluids. Rob had spent the night back and forth between the two bedrooms, nervously looking for improvement. He had found none. They slept deeply and silently barely moving. He stood chewing his thumbnail watching from the doorway of Rebecca's room. He was worried to the point of nausea. Eventually, he gave in and went to bed. He drifted into an unsettled sleep, tossing and turning and wrestling with the quilt. Finally, his subconscious mind took over and he drifted into a deep dreamlike state.

He sank into the strange world of unreality, a happy escape from the terrible state of affairs he currently found himself in. He was in the middle of a beautiful sunken garden the perfume of the roses was heady and intoxicating. He could feel the warm sun's rays on his skin and his spirits were light and carefree as on any summer's day. He knew where he was instantly. Abbot's Wood – James' house. He walked lightly almost floating above the path. He speeded up as he reached the door to the house. It opened before him and he floated into the hallway. He found himself in the drawing room among the maps and the papers, the remains of an afternoon tea tray on the table. His heart leapt for joy as he saw the back of a man, slightly balding but strong and in his early thirties. He turned around to greet Rob.

"What errors have been made my old friend?" he said.

His broad face was edged with spectacular whiskers, creating a distinguished look, the surprised arched eyebrows were raised even more today and his nut-brown eyes were dulled with sadness.

"We lost the chalice. Silas stole it while we slept… and Nate and my sister are dreadfully ill and George too… there is only us now."

"I am here but for a brief moment Rob, I can but try to come to you when you are wakened, but time is twisted so I do not know when."

"We never thought we would see you again."

"You should not have seen me more. We had visited through my lifetime and it was spent, but now time is wrong and changes are being made which must be reversed. We must set our minds to finding the chalice once more – though this time we have now clues, no assistance!"

"Where can we look? John Stell the monk said the chalice is only powerful close to the abbey, so that must mean it is hidden nearby?"

"We must seek the chalice when you are fully woken… this is not the real world. This is a world built on imaginings and dreams, a counterfeit world which is unreliable…"

Rob looked down in disappointment.

James moved towards him kindly. He put his hands on his shoulders and looked sternly into his eyes.

"Never give in… it seems challenging today, but we will overcome and rise above it… *'semper sursum'* – remember – always rising – we will overcome!"

Rob smiled. 'Semper sursum' was the Latin motto Ramsden had chosen for Barrow.

As the two smiled at each other the room lost definition and a grey blankness descended. James drifted away slowly and Rob felt his consciousness being wrenched back to his earthly body. With a violent slam he returned and awoke. Every cell of his body burned and pained him and he gasped for breath as surely as if he had been drowning. Unwanted tears spilled down his cheeks and he was overcome with an overwhelming melancholy. He was back and there was work to do.

He lay on the bed breathing rapidly and his T-shirt was damp with sweat. This had been no normal dream; he had been transported from his own body. He showered and got ready to resume the search. He looked in on Nate and Rebecca they were still sleeping a heavy and unnatural sleep. Mum didn't seem too worried now they had seen the Doctor explaining that the best cure for a virus was lots of rest. Rob didn't say anything but he knew that they would not get better until the chalice was returned.

He took the car this time and drove up to Abbot's Wood and parked. He did not relish the walk through the quiet wood. It seemed particularly lonely today. The muddy paths were edged with decaying leaves and the undergrowth was tangled and matted. The stillness was unnerving and he was compelled to look over his shoulder to check he was not being followed. He carried on towards the rear of the wood along the main path. Suddenly he heard a faint fluttering and spun around quickly. A solitary magpie alighted on the high branch of a sycamore tree. He stared at it, willing it to fly away. Rob trudged onwards, past the remnants of the Precinct wall, ivy covered and worn. He started to jog, he didn't know why but he felt safer. The quicker he ran the better he felt, until he was running as though his life depended on it. He broke away from the path and into the trees. He caught glimpses of the abbey below, nestled in the valley, resting quietly like an old lady in her chair.

As he ran on the weather began to change. Clouds reeled in from the sea and the skies darkened. The hairs on the back of Rob's neck prickled, warning him of imminent danger. He felt vulnerable on the pathway and he veered off into the trees. As he ran the branches clawed at his clothes and the wind whipped up fiercely. He was as alert and as nervous as a hunted fox. His hoody caught on brambles and he pulled the fabric roughly away, as he managed to release it he stumbled and unexpectedly a frantic flapping of wings rose in front of him, causing him to lose his balance completely. He protected his face with his arms as the beating wings caught him full on. He managed to roll forwards into the undergrowth, falling into a small passage way. He jumped to his feet and ran rapidly down the path. He ran faster and faster, not knowing where he was going, deeper into the wood, until the trench curved into a more obvious passage.

Ahead lay a bridge across the channel. The woods shimmered and sparked. He knew by now something was happening. A rattling and pounding noise arose from the right of the bridge and four black horses thudded across, drawing a coach behind them. He was astounded. It sped towards the direction he had come from and he caught a glimpse of the passengers. It was James and his wife. Rob ducked quickly beneath the bridge so he would not be seen. He continued down the track way, which was now more defined and well used. He soon reached the back of the house, it was clear that the track was designed to keep the servants and tradesmen out of view from the big house. Indeed he noticed a familiar figure walking towards him, carrying a basket. It was Miss Sheriff. She was more smartly dressed than the first time he had seen her and slightly older.

"What are you doing here? I thought we had seen the last of you when you disappeared so quickly."

"Er... I'm not sure, things have gone wrong... George is ill and we've lost the chalice... and my brother and sister are ill too... Silas Dixon has the chalice!"

She stood quietly and considered the problem. She grabbed him by the arm and led him towards the kitchens.

"You must see Sir James immediately," she said decisively.

They walked towards the door and Miss Sheriff opened the door quietly and peeped inside, checking who was there. They went inside and down a small passage. There were a number of coats hanging from the hooks on the wall. She removed one and handed it to him.

"Put this on, you will be less conspicuous."

He did as he was told and put it on. It was far too big but he felt less obvious dressed in the coat. She led him into a large kitchen. A maid was washing dishes in the large stone sink and another woman was making pastry on the well-scrubbed table. It reminded him of George's mother and their kitchen. Not many modern conveniences here he thought. Lee pulled out a chair and nodded to him to sit.

The two servants looked curiously at him but were obviously in some awe of Miss Sheriff.

"This young man is here to see Sir James, I will tell him he is here." She swept out closing the door behind her. Rob was uncomfortable under the curious gaze of the cook. She carried on with her task but glanced at him every few minutes. He avoided her eyes and looked down at the floor as though something very interesting was compelling him to do so.

After what seemed like ages Miss Sheriff returned.

"Sir James will see you now. Follow me!"

He did as he was told once more and followed her through a maze of hallways and passages. They walked across an impressively tiled hallway, some with ram's heads emblazoned on them. Rob smirked, again evidence of Ramsden's sense of self-worth. The large oak door was opened for them and they were ushered into the room they had been in previously. James was leaning against the ornate fireplace, his face reflected in the mirror above. As he caught sight of them he lit up with excitement.

"My boy! It is so good to see you again!" he cried. He rushed towards the boy and embraced like an old friend.

Rob was unsure how advanced in years he was on this encounter, but he looked similar to when they had found the chalice.

"I did not think to see you so soon, I trust all is well? I had strange dreams last night of the chalice and you… " he trailed off and his expression suggested he was suddenly aware of the problem. His face grew stern and his eyes searched for the answer on Rob's face.

"It's not good news James, not by any stretch of the imagination. We have lost the chalice."

James was crestfallen and the colour drained from his usually ruddy cheeks.

"But we have only just found it… how could this happen?" he demanded.

Rob sat down heavily on the chair and related the events, as far as he could. He wondered if the other things he had experienced had already been erased from the timeline. It was mightily confusing and he could hardly tell James he had seen him as a very old man.

"The old monk said that the chalice is only powerful close to the abbey-do you think we can find it? What if it isn't in my time?" He caught his breath.

James looked thoughtfully at him. Miss Sheriff had not moved and as they considered the room wavered and crackled. Rob leapt to his feet. This was happening too quickly, he hadn't had time to talk to James. This must be a result of Silas Dixon's conjuring. Without another thought he grabbed hold of James by the arm and hung onto him. The room span and once more he was transported to another time, but this time he had taken James with him.

CHAPTER 19

OLD FRIENDS

They landed with a bump, almost knocking someone over.

"God's Blood! Where hast thou come from?" cried a vaguely familiar voice.

The young man stood up and straightened his tricorn hat. As he focused and saw Rob his mouth fell open in surprise.

"'Tis thee… young Rob! Well I ne'er thought to see thee again in this life!"

Rob winced. Yet again Tom addressed him as though he was a young boy instead of a boy of his own age.

"Tom!"

"Aye 'tis me!" Tom grinned, "And what perils art thou in now? I thought we had vanquished the evil one – surely nought can be amiss?"

James was as stiff as an ironing board, he had not moved since they had landed so abruptly on top of Tom. His face was immobile and his eyes were as round as dishes.

"Er… this is James… erm Sir James actually, Sir James Ramsden, mayor of Barrow, James – this is Tom… er…" Rob was at a loss to tell him Tom's surname.

"Tom RALLISON, Customs Officer for Rampside, at your service your Lordship!" he emphasised the Rallison and bowed with a flourish to James.

James merely blinked.

Rob felt pity. He understood how strange it was when you first slipped out of time. He patted him on the shoulder.

"It's alright James, you'll get used to this… we are in another time," he glanced around him, "and place by the look of it."

"Another time… how will we return to…" the words stuck in his throat.

Rob shrugged and this was echoed by Tom.

"Worry not Sir, things will right themselves. 'Tis mightily disturbing but thou shall become accustomed to it. So why art thou here?" he addressed Rob again.

"We have lost a great treasure and the power it holds is changing time and we have to find it to put it right. Nate and my sister are ill and they will not be safe until it's found. But I don't know why we're here… your treasure – the sword – is still safe."

Tom looked thoughtful and he took off his hat. He was suddenly taking charge and bade them follow him.

It was only now that they were able to take in their surroundings properly. They were on the roadside, which really resembled a dirt track more than a road. Tom led them onward past fields and hedgerows, the wind blowing from the sea. Behind them was the coast and from this the distance they could see Piel and the other isles. Ahead was countryside, with few buildings.

They marched on past the squat church of St Michael and on down the road towards Barrow.

"Thou said yon man is Mayor of Barrow?" Tom hissed quietly to Rob.

"Yeah he is!"

"Barrow? 'Tis a meagre village with no more than 150 souls – he must be the local madman if he thinks he be mayor!" he shot a wary glance at poor James, who did not look his usual commanding self in this situation.

"He is from Victorian times," explained Rob.

Tom looked blankly.

"I mean… he lives in… 1880 something… you know the 19th century."

Tom looked askance and then nodded.

A small group of cottages appeared on the brow of the hill. Moorhead. The cottages were simple and smoke meandered from the chimneys. Small strips of cultivated land surrounded them and chickens ran free in the dusty yard. Washing blew, billowing in the wind like sails and children played in the yard. A small grubby boy, dressed in breeches and shirt and with no shoes on his dirty feet ran up to Tom excitedly.

Tom lifted the child and threw him above his head, making him giggle. He held him and gave him a rough hug.

"Ha my lad, hast tha been good for thy mother?" Tom said.

The child giggled and snuggled into his father's shoulder. Rob looked on surprised. Tom seemed young to have a child, but he remembered Nate had told him that Dolly was expecting a child when they had last seen him.

"This is my boy… Nathaniel," Tom informed them. "He will be four in the summer."

Rob smiled and pointed at the boy.

"Aye we named him for thy brother," Tom confirmed what Rob was silently thinking.

On cue a young woman appeared at the doorway. She was a striking young lady with hair like burnished gold, unruly wisps of hair escaping from her white cap. She was short and slight, but with a formidable attitude, which showed in her determined heart shaped face.

"So Tom, thou hast fetched visitors with thee?"

"Aye and they have travelled some way," he replied wryly.

James nodded politely and Rob smiled. He had never met Dolly, but had heard all about her from Nate.

The all trooped into the cottage behind her. It was simple, clean and tidy, with even less in the way of comforts than George's house and distinctly less than Abbot's Wood.

They were waved towards the roughly hewn bench on one side of the table. It was well worn, old and polished with a high back and carved sides. They sat down as they had been bidden and rested against the large wooden table. A large fire burned in a wide grate with various cooking pots suspended above it. Dolly poured a golden liquid from an earthenware jug into large glass tumblers. The glass was opaque and crude but very similar to those, which Rob drank from at home. Both strangers sipped the liquid cautiously. It was thick and cloyingly sweet with a distinct taste of apples.

"Splendid cider Madame," acknowledged James politely.

Rob raised his eyebrows; it tasted much stronger than any cider he had ever tasted.

"So Tom, who do we have visiting us on this fine day?" asked Dolly.

"Dolly, thou will not believe it… but this," indicating Rob, "is young Nate's brother… dost thou remember… the one with the great roaring horseless carriage?"

The memory of the day they travelled in Rob's car rushed back and the dawn of recognition spread across her face.

"Ah that I do… and where is Nate? Has he not come with thee?"

She said this as though it was the most natural thing in the world to travel back and forth through time.

"No, not this time, I'm afraid he is… not well," said Rob.

They sat around the simple table and talked about the difficulties facing Rob and Sir James. Dolly was slightly star struck at having a mayor in her kitchen; people of his stature were held in great esteem in her day.

The hours drew on and there was no sign of them being whisked back to their timelines. Dusk fell as the dying sun sank into the west and very soon the farm was covered with darkness. Tom lit the candles, but most of the light came from the fire. Dolly busied herself making them supper and putting the child to bed. He was placed in a box bed in the loft above the main room and Rob wondered if, like when he was a child, he was afraid of the dark because it certainly seemed a lot darker here than at home. Supper over, they returned to the discussion about what they could do to retrieve the treasure.

"There must be a reason you are both sent here to us – it cannot be chance. When we met with you before, our paths crossed to allow us to save the sword did they not?" remarked Tom.

"He may well have something Rob. I'll wager there is a way to find the chalice by being here," agreed James.

"But what? What clues can there be here? After all… it will be another hundred or more years from now that we find the chalice with Miss Sheriff… so how can it help… ?"

Suddenly, like a light bulb going on Rob realised just how useful it would be to be thrown into a much earlier time.

"Oh my God! That's the point!" he cried, "The chalice is still hidden – they don't know we are here and they don't know where we found it! We can find it again… but sooner… much sooner!" His face broke into a big grin.

James slapped his knee and laughed heartily.

"By God! I think you're right! We have the chance to rescue it again and keep it from those devils. We can yet save your sister and brother… and fulfil our promise to the old monk." The years dropped away from him and the old James beamed through.

"We must repair to where you found this chalice… on the morrow," Tom declared.

"Where was the place?" enquired Dolly.

"It was at Parkhouse farm, in the well Madame," James said politely.

Tom and Dolly exchanged a glance, which suggested this would be a problem.

"Er… what's up?" Rob said.

"Up? What dost thou mean?"

"Er… I mean… is that a problem?"

"'Tis not the best place to visit, I'll warrant!" confirmed Tom.

James groaned.

"Why?"

"Rob, thou knowest I am the revenue man for this place?"

Rob nodded.

"So this means I come into contact with many rogues and vagabonds… and I have to tell thee that he who dwells at that farm is one such scoundrel. 'Twill be no easy matter to get thee into the dairy without attracting his attention. They do say he is a necromancer and evil doer and has much cunning."

They all fell silent.

"Well let's to bed, it may look better in the light of day," said Dolly. "We have but one bed above, but we can find thee a straw mattress from the barn…" she caught sight of James' look of horror and added, "Your Lordship can sleep upon the settle, I can give thee some blankets and a pillow to make thee comfortable."

Neither of them was comfortable, both were unsettled and worried about the task that lay ahead. It seemed to Rob that it would never be over. Each time they thought they had won the day something went wrong.

The temperature dropped as the night drew on and Rob wondered how people survived during this era. He concluded that they were very hardy! His eyelids began to close and although he was cold he was tired. Just as he was about to drift off into sleep a loud scratching noise came from beside the dying embers of the fire. He heard it again and his eyes opened slowly-dreading what he would see. The scratching turned into a scurrying and within seconds there was screaming. A small mouse ran speedily across the room and over the rough blanket covering Rob. He leapt up and woke the household with his yelling. James nearly fell off the settle and the little boy cried. Tom rushed down the wooden ladder in his nightshirt expecting intruders. When he discovered what the problem was he howled with laughter. Mice were part of everyday life in the eighteenth century and certainly nothing to shout about.

Morning came sooner than Rob had hoped. The disturbed night met an early dawn start and he was drained of all energy. He had a wash with cold water from the outside pump using a piece of foul smelling soap which he wouldn't have washed his dog with. The only benefit was that the cold water woke him up. James was less shocked at the arrangements for personal hygiene, having only benefitted from the luxury of a bathroom and running water in his later years. Once they had breakfasted upon some very gritty bread and cheese they turned to organising their plan to retrieve the treasure once again.

"We must be careful not to alert yon farmer that he holds something precious, or 'twill be God's own task to prevent him from keeping it," he said.

"Is there no other way we can get into the well, other than through the dairy?" enquired James.

"There may well be – but I know of none… though there be tales that the secret passages which lead to Piel do connect with the farm."

"There is a way," announced Dolly who was listening to the discussion.

The three men looked at her in expectation.

"My father… he knows of many of the tunnels… from his time with Swarbrick and his gang – the smugglers knew all the places to hide and stow away booty," she blushed at the shameful remembrance.

Tom nodded and grinned.

"I had not thought on't! This will be our best course – he can guide us to the best place and wouldst not dare speak on't now he is father-in-law to the Preventive man for the district."

"Of course any help would be useful, it is a great pity I have no access to my maps and plans in this time," added James.

"Art thou coming with us your Lordship?" asked Tom, a little amazed.

"Tom... desist from calling me your Lordship... here in your time I am just as you, an ordinary man. My name is James. Plus... where else would I go? I would be foolish to leave Rob as we travelled here together and our fates are locked. Where he goes I must go too."

Tom nodded, but did not look convinced.

They gathered up provisions to take with them, which Tom stuffed into a leather bag. They moved towards the door to leave when suddenly Dolly blocked their way.

"I will be with thee too. My father will not easily help thee without my persuasion. The child will be well looked after by Susannah, one more bairn will not harm."

"Thou can come to see thy father but no more," warned Tom.

Dolly set her face into a defiant stare, raising an eyebrow.

"I think Thomas that thou knowest, I *will* be with thee for the whole journey. I have seen greater dangers than these and survived."

Tom opened his mouth to protest, but something about his wife's demeanour stopped him from saying more.

Rob chuckled to himself. Dolly was a feisty one; no wonder his female family members had determined characters if this was their ancestress. He looked at her closely, recognising some startling similarities to his mum and sister. You wouldn't want to cross her that was for sure. Maybe feminism wasn't that new after all?

CHAPTER 20

A NEW QUEST AND OLD ADVERSARIES

They trekked across muddy fields for about a mile to the small village of Rampside. Rob was completely lost; he could not see any landmarks that he recognised. James spoke little and worried furrows crossed his brow as they walked. He was deep in thought and Rob could appreciate how he felt. He was becoming more used to the rapid transition from one time to another but he remembered clearly, his panic when it first happened. So much had passed and yet they were no nearer to rescuing the chalice than they had been. They approached the coast and both newcomers suddenly recognised where they were. The medieval fortress rose ahead of them at Piel and they could see the embracing arms of Walney Island across the narrow channel which would become so important in the development of Barrow in the future. James stopped to mop his brow with a large pocket-handkerchief. He gazed across the glimmering water to the headland at Barrow Village. The scene was rural and green, with only random houses dotted here and there. Roa Island to the south was a small isolated island between the mainland and Piel, unconnected by the causeway, which both James and Rob knew. Of course James had known this place well. It had been where the Furness Railway Company had first landed their locomotive.

They walked on until they reached a small and tumbledown inn. John Jackson, Dolly's father was the innkeeper of this dilapidated establishment. His trade had diminished since he had turned his back on petty thievery and smuggling and he was no better tempered for it. He had been ashamed of his weakness and regretted placing his young daughter in danger, but he could not help but blame Tom. If he had not taken a fancy to Dolly, the business would be continuing. Instead he scraped a poor living running the alehouse, brewing beer to sell locally and making deliveries of goods and produce with his horse and cart. He was a bitter and disappointed man, alone since his wife had perished at Dolly's birth. Some men thrive on adversity while others give into their weak character, blaming all but themselves for their fate. John Jackson was of the latter persuasion.

There was no warm welcome for Dolly as she entered her old home. Jackson was alone in the inn, lamenting his poor luck and smoking a clay pipe. Grey smoke wove a crooked halo around his head. He was unkempt and had a grey pallor, with dark circles beneath his eyes. He was seated in a wooden chair beside the fire and made no move to greet them as they came in. He perked up a little when he saw they were not alone and stood to serve the prospective customers.

"Nay we need no ale John, we have come to talk with thee," Tom said.

"Aye well, thou hast killed my trade so I would not think thou would bring me custom!" he grumbled.

"Father... let it be... 'tis nigh on five years, be glad thou art still alive to tell the tale!" answered Dolly shortly.

He sighed heavily.

James read the situation perfectly and took charge.

"My good man, we have some questions to ask. You will be well paid... if you answer them properly."

The others glanced in astonishment.

Jackson straightened his posture and a small avaricious smile curled across his face.

"Aye... we need thy help... but 'tis a secret undertaking, thou can say nought of this," added Tom, joining in.

Tom told him the briefest details because he did not altogether trust him. The old man, for he was above fifty, ran his hand through his greasy hair. He considered for a moment and retreated to another room. Within moments he returned with a roll of maps. These charts were as old, worn and grubby as he was himself. He rolled them onto the table, holding them down with a candleholder and an iron pot. He stroked the parchment flat and pored over it, as though it was a precious treasure. The maps were all ages and sizes, some were sea charts and others maps showing mine workings and villages. Jackson pointed with a gnarled and dirty finger tracing his way around the places shown on the map. He hesitated and then stabbed one hard, jabbing it with his fingernail.

They looked closely and could see some places they recognised. The abbey was prominent and the farm they were interested in was clearly drawn. Track ways and lanes meandered across the paper like a spider's web and they tried hard to make sense of what they were seeing. Then, Rob recognised the name Boulton's Common. He gasped with surprise. This was where he lived – he remembered being told that the house was built on common land and the name rang a bell immediately. The whole of the area was fields and agricultural land. Some way below the common was a Blacksmith's and another farm but not the one they sought, further towards the abbey was Parkhouse Grange... this was the farm. Jackson pointed to the fields and a dotted line meandered from just above the common to the farm itself, another led away from the farm to the abbey and joined with a third from abbey to the coast and onto Piel.

"So it is true! There is a tunnel from the abbey. I know Nate said he had been in it, but I thought he was exaggerating," cried Rob.

"Aye of course 'tis true silly lad!" said the innkeeper, "They monks were master builders and engineers. 'Twas no effort for them to make tunnels for mining... and smuggling."

Rob was a little annoyed at his dismissive comment,

even if he was his great, great, great… granddad.

"The monks were honourable men! They surely did not smuggle!" argued Sir James.

"Aye that they did yer honour… they was great smugglers. Why dost tha think they built yon castle?" he waved towards Piel, "'Twas a great storehouse, fortified and they ran wool out and wine and brandy in… they were not for paying the King's duty on't and rightly so!"

James looked scandalised and Rob thought it probably was true, after all they had become the second richest abbey in the land and corruption was one reason for the Dissolution. Tom shook his head in disgust and privately thought if he had been the Preventive man in those days they would not have got away with it.

"If thou art clever, tha canst slip into the farm without bein' seen. If tha uses the tunnel

that leads from the abbey. 'Tis simple, these tunnels have long been used and 'tis not so long since Swarbrick used 'em so they'll be shored up and safe," Jackson seemed excited by the prospect. His eyes glinted greedily at the thought of what he might gain from this venture.

He lifted a trap door in the floor, sending the dust and debris of months flying across the flagstones and into the air. Dolly coughed and waved her hand in front of her face.

"I see thou dost not value cleaning over much Father!"

Jackson grinned, "There be only me girl, why would

I waste time on sweeping, the customers I get don't bother with fripperies."

She coughed again and looked sadly at the old man.

He scuttled down into the cavernous cellar, where she and Tom had been imprisoned by the smugglers once. He returned with a length of rope and two old lanterns. He was evidently keen to help them in their enterprise.

Tom took the lanterns from him and passed one to Rob, as he reached for the rope the old chap slung it over his own shoulder. He stood with the same determined look his daughter had displayed earlier.

"What are you doing John? We must be on our way," asked Tom guessing the answer.

"I be coming with ye! We can use the cart… and I do know where the entrance is to the tunnel," he paused, his expression mournful. "An' I want to make amends to thee and Dolly; I swear I can be of assistance."

Tom and Dolly looked at each other. Dolly's expression melted a little and Tom had not the heart to deny his request.

"Ah well, the more the merrier I suppose," said James.

"Aye well, if thou canst go at thy age, then I will too!" added Jackson.

James blustered and his colour reddened in indignation.

It was a bumpy ride to the abbey, past Parkhouse Grange. The rickety old cart was pulled by an old brown and white horse that appeared to be in no particular hurry. Rob did wonder at one point whether it would be quicker to walk. He and Tom were seated on sacks in the back while Dolly and Sir James were perched on the seat at the front, driven by John Jackson. They rattled along the muddy track to Roose village, which was no more than a few houses, past the Smithy on the hill, which Rob recognised as where the fish and chip shop was in his day. The smith was hard at work and waved when he saw Jackson.

"You thrown your lot in with the law now Jack? Or hast the Preventive man caught up with thee at last?" he laughed heartily.

"Nay, I be taking these folk up to Dalton... 'tis market day tha knows!" The lies rolled from his tongue as easily as the waves on the beach, but at least he had not revealed the true reason for their journey.

"An... they paid good coin fer it!" he added for good measure.

"Tha's an owld maggoty reprobate! Dost tha charge thy own kin?" the smith called after him.

Jackson shrugged and flicked the reins to encourage the horse onwards.

He chuckled as they rode on up the track. Tom shook his head in disbelief

They drove past a sprawling farm at the bottom of the hill, a meadow full of colourful wild flowers lay in front of it and the stream could be seen glistening as it wound its way through the valley. James commented on the absence of his railway and both he and Rob recognised

Bow Bridge as they rumbled past. They drew near to the old cottage across from the abbey. It looked very different. It was surrounded by a garden with vegetables, chickens ran free on the dusty yard in front and there were more trees. Rob thought it looked like the picture on a chocolate box. The abbey was open and unfenced, but covered with invasive green ivy. Walls rose where there were none, it was overgrown and the stonework hardly visible in some parts, but even in the midst of its unkempt chaos it was still magnificent.

Jackson lit up his foul smelling clay pipe and wandered over to the cottager who was working in the garden. The two exchanged words for a few minutes and a boy appeared from behind the cottage and unhitched the horse. He led it to some outbuildings alongside and out of sight. Jackson took the lantern and rope and nodded to Tom to do the same. They followed him and walked away from the amphitheatre and straight into the abbey grounds.

Rob felt a bit guilty, it seemed wrong to be able to access it so easily… and for free. He was astonished to see the abbey in this state. The vegetation was covering it and great heaps of stone lay around, where people had begun to remove it for building work elsewhere. The abbey looked brighter and newer. He mused that they only had a fleeting impression of its beauty and impressiveness in his day and not for the first time wondered what it must have looked like when in use.

They walked along the rear of the infirmary and up into

the abbot's lodgings, greatly overgrown with brambles and ivy. The old man led them towards the river, choked with weeds but running fast. He jumped down the banking; shadows from the abbey church falling across the stream and making them feel cold. A double arched tunnel only a few feet high opened into the bank above and disappeared towards the way they had come.

He pulled away some of the undergrowth and revealed the opening. He ducked down and went in bent double.

"Come then! We have not the whole day, the tunnel fills at certain times and we must be clear by then."

They obediently jumped into the stream, which thankfully was low as it was summer. Jackson had disappeared into the tunnel ahead of them, Tom led Dolly next and James reluctantly followed, mourning the damage this would do to his smart leather boots. Rob brought up the rear. Jackson and Tom lit the lanterns; Rob followed the pale light glowing ahead. The tunnel opened wider as they travelled through and the water was shallow. The air was sour and dank and nobody spoke as they walked on. The walls dripped and were coated with black slime, which was not an encouraging sight. Rob recalled the mouse of last night and hoped there would be nothing larger down here. Apart from the meagre light from the lanterns everywhere was palled in thick blackness and silence fell upon them like a cloak. They had been walking for about five minutes, hampered by the dark and water sloshing around their feet, when the tunnel opened into an underground vault. At least here they could stand up. They rested momentarily and could see that other tunnels converged upon this space. They would have found it difficult to orientate and decide which one to take had Jackson not been with them.

He veered left and they bent low once more, backs aching and knees cramping, but at least they were on their way. Rob reasoned there could not be too far to go if it was a straight line to the farm; it only took fifteen minutes to walk there normally. The tunnel rose slightly and an arch opened in front of them. Rob and James grew excited and pointed at the keystone. On it was carved a sprig of leaves and berries… just as they had seen at the farm… so long ago. The others looked curiously at their animated faces…

"It's the nightshade… the sign for the chalice! We can't be far from the farm," cried Rob.

"Well, soft lad, we're in the tunnel that links the abbey to the farm. Just ahead is the bottom of the well tha's been on about!"

Cries of approval echoed around the passage.

"Aye… but tha must be quiet… unless tha wants 'im above to catch on!"

"Who is 'im …? I mean he?" enquired Rob.

"Why owld Dixon… farmer… he's a bigger miscreant than me… and a greedy cove too, 'tis said he dabbles in't dark arts. If he guesses tha knows where gold lies tha's done for!"

Rob and James paled. Dixon? It couldn't be?

"Dixon? What is his other name?"

"Silas… Silas the snake we calls 'im."

"It can't be the same Silas Dixon we defeated! He hails from thy time does he not?" asked Tom.

"I don't know… nothing would surprise me!"

Dolly took charge. She brought them back to the job in hand and insisted they decide who was to go forward to retrieve the chalice.

"This tunnel must lead to the well… as thou said. So who is to go? You did say 'twas cramped… I am the smallest so I do believe 'should be me."

"Nay, lass thou canst not go… 'twould not be safe!" her father insisted.

"I'll go," said Rob.

"Well, so be it… but I shall be behind thee," said Tom.

They were about to set off through the archway when Dolly slipped past them faster than an eel and just as slippery. Tom cried out, anguished that his wife was putting herself in danger. He grabbed the lantern and followed her with Rob fast on his tail. As they moved forward the tunnel shrank in size and it was dark as night. They soon caught up with Dolly but could not persuade her to return to where James and her father waited. They pressed on and could hear the sound of water running ahead of them. The tunnel diminished to a very tight space and ahead they could see a curved wall. They ascertained that this must be the well. There appeared to be some kind of lever and pulley system to allow entrance from the well to the tunnel.

The space in the passage was very narrow and both men

had to stop. Dolly had been right. She was the only one who would fit. She pushed her way through, her long skirt dragging in the mud and water. Rob realised that she was approaching the place where the chalice lay from the other direction to which George had come from. As she reached the well wall she peered around looking up and down for the sign. Suddenly, she cried out.

"There's a carving… it's the same as the one on the arch."

"Brilliant! Try and release the stone. George told us the chalice was behind it…"

The words dried up almost before they were out. At the same time Dolly reached above her and touched the stone. There was a rumble and a flash of light and her hand touched another hand. Rob froze and he could hardly be more astonished. An ethereal shape crawled through the newly opened door into the well. It was George.

"George!" yelled Rob.

The boy seemed not to see him. Dolly had not moved. Tom was silent behind him. It looked like a tableau in a wax museum. As George moved the stone it revealed a gap from which something heavy fell, hitting him on the forehead. Dolly moved her hand and pressed the brick. The brick slid back – just as if George had not moved it at all. The object fell and she caught it deftly. The air vibrated and Rob was overcome by dizziness. He watched as George faded and Dolly reanimated. The chalice was in their hands at last.

What he had seen was the reversal of the other discovery. They had altered time by retrieving the treasure in an earlier time. He wondered if this had changed things in his century too. He certainly hoped so. Dolly scrambled back to where they crouched and gestured them to move out. They returned to where Jackson and James were patiently waiting. The excitement was overwhelming, James was delighted and even Jackson smiled.

"Well ye have what ye came for… we'd best get on and get thee back home," said Jackson.

They made their way back through the tunnel in silence. Their prize was safe, but they all recognised the feelings of apprehension and anti-climax.

They emerged from the culvert they had started from, a lot dirtier and more dishevelled than they had been earlier. The light made them wince as they came into the abbey again. They climbed up onto the bank and sat down for a moment to rest. Dolly unrolled the wrapping from the chalice and it glinted in the sun. It was remarkably shiny for something that had been concealed underground for so long. The cawing of magpies echoed around the high walls of the church like an alarm. Dolly wrapped it up quickly again and Rob's eyes darted around to see where the birds were. He sincerely hoped they did not signify danger as they did in his time, but he already knew the answer in his heart. The sun warmed them quickly and their wet shoes and clothes began to dry, but they did not feel the comfort of it. It only took them minutes to return to the cart.

Dolly jumped into the back and hid the treasure beneath the old sacks and sat down on top of it. So she was aware of the danger too! The cackling of the magpies travelled through the warm air from the trees making the hair on the back of Rob's neck stand on end. He wanted to get away as speedily as they could. Jackson had gone to the yard to retrieve his horse and was leading it back to hitch it to the cart. He faltered for a moment and then pulled the reins to lead the old nag on. James climbed up to the seat in front but Rob stood firmly by the cart.

From behind the cottage a figure appeared. He was a familiar figure, the balding head and hawk like nose, tall and imposing, but dressed in coat and britches as any self-respecting farmer of the eighteenth century would be. It was Silas Dixon, in the flesh.

As he drew nearer Rob's blood ran cold. The man stopped close by the cart and Dolly shuffled uncomfortably, spreading her muddy skirt to ensure the chalice was hidden.

"What brings thee here Jackson? Up to no good I'll warrant!" he sneered.

Rob looked at him closely. He did not appear to recognise him.

"Not that it be any business of thine... we bin t' market at Dalton and took our ease here," retorted Jackson.

"Humph!" grunted Silas. "Well where's thy wares then? Or was the market sold out? An' didst tha fall in Mill Beck on thy way?" He looked them up and down, noticing their wet and muddy clothes.

"Aye… that's just about reet!" chortled Jackson, "We'll be on our way, can't be dilly dallying with thee Silas."

With that he jumped up on the cart and beckoned Tom and Rob to do the same. Silas stared at them, his face unreadable. Behind him a magpie landed on the gatepost and cackled noisily, trying to attract his attention.

John Jackson snapped the reins twice and whistled, the old nag startled into motion. They rolled along the lane innocently. Dolly was red faced and her blood ran hot and cold for fear of discovery. It was as though the chalice was crying out to be found; she spread her skirts more widely to obscure the sacking beneath which the chalice lay. Dixon watched them leave and was still observing them as they turned the corner into the edge of the woodland covering the edges of Beckan's Gill.

Nobody spoke or breathed until they were out of sight.

"That was close!" gasped Rob, "I was sure he would ask us what was in the cart."

"Aye 'twas a tense moment, I'm sure that magpie was speaking to him – vile creature!"

As she spoke two flew above them and dived in an out of the trees. Tom waved his hat at them to shoo them away and as he did so a sleek black raven glided down from the higher branches and cut through the air between them. They screeched raucously and flapped their wings furiously to escape from the huge bird. He landed lightly on the end of the cart like a lone sentry. The group were heartened by his arrival.

Onward they went until they reached Tom's cottage at

Moorhead. Jackson drove off the track and into the makeshift courtyard at the side. He untethered the old horse and Tom led him to the water trough in the yard by the pump. Jackson stood uneasily as the others got down from the cart and made their way to the cottage. Nathaniel, Dolly's young son ran from where he had been playing in the dirt with the other children and reached up to be lifted. Jackson bowed his head. This was his first encounter with his little grandson. Dolly smiled and beckoned him to follow.

As they reached the door she handed the boy to him and said, "Meet thy grandson... Nathaniel." The boy laughed and reached out a chubby hand to him. Jackson took it in his bear like paw and shook it gently.

"Thy Ma would have been proud... he's a bonny lad."

They all retired inside and Dolly set to making food for her guests. The chalice was revealed and placed on the table for the time being.

Very soon they were sharing bowls of pottage, which Dolly had left simmering on the hearth. It was like a lumpy soup or stew, with no meat to be found. It consisted of leeks, cabbage and onions, there was a hint of wild garlic and herbs but the flavour was fairly bland never the less. It was eaten with hunks of rough bread, which tasted a little gritty to Rob, but he could not deny that it was quite filling.

When they had finished they discussed the next plan of attack. This must involve returning Rob and James to their own times. They had to remove the threat of the Silas they had just met from stealing the chalice back. Tom suggested they rest for the night and see what they could work out the next day. Neither James nor Rob was very keen on this idea, but there seemed to be no alternative. They said goodbye to Dolly's father and as he turned to leave she pecked him on the cheek. He smiled and acknowledged her gesture. Rob was pleased that they had now put aside their differences and were friends again. He knew from his own experience that life was too short to harbour grudges and nurse old wounds.

They had settled down to sleep when Rob was disturbed again. A scrambling noise outside awoke James as well. Someone was outside. Instinctively, James wrapped up the chalice in sacking and clutched it to his chest.

"Who is it?" he whispered, "Can you espy through the window?"

Rob peered through the streaky glass.

He jumped back quickly. It was not a sight he had hoped to see again. The night gargoyles were even more potent and evil in this century it seemed to him. They were scraping around the yard and in the outbuildings and across the yard he could see Silas silhouetted against the moonlight. He shivered involuntarily.

Tom climbed down from the loft room and was in the process of dressing. He looked dishevelled and concerned. Rob put a finger to his lips to silence him.

James indicated that he had the chalice safe. The three crept to the side of the wall away from the small window. Rob was glad for the first time that eighteenth century houses did not have large windows. A whispered conversation ensued and the three decided what to do next.

Tom beckoned them into the small scullery at the back of the cottage. He glanced through the even tinier window to see if the creatures were about. All was quiet and the small cottage garden was empty. They carefully opened the scullery door and slipped silently into the night. They made their way across the field and away from the cottage. James was between them but he struggled to keep up their pace. The ground was uneven and had it not been for the bright moon casting its silver light they would have found it impossible to find their way. Tom knew the land well and steered them towards the coast. The Concle was the only place he could think of in which to lay low. They reached the path along the edge of the cliff and ran as fast as they could along it, dragging poor James with them.

"By God! I doubt I have been required to use this much energy since I was supervising the building of the railway. I trust we will reach the destination soon… or I will surely expire?"

"We are close by… keep moving… we are easy spotted here and dawn will soon be breaking," encouraged Tom.

They clambered over rough ground and emerged at the

old inn. Its brooding presence did nothing to encourage them but they pushed on any way. Tom pounded on the door as hard as he could. They waited for what seemed ages until they heard Jackson cursing behind the door.

"'Tis me, Tom! Let us enter!" he demanded.

The door flew open revealing a surprised John Jackson.

"I had not thought to see thee this soon lad!"

"Nor I you! But we are sore pressed. Let us come in!"

They entered the inn and Jackson slammed shut the door behind them.

He picked up his tallow candle, which spat and spewed smoke from its wick. They stumbled through to the main room and collapsed onto the chairs and benches. James pulled out the handkerchief to wipe his brow. His breathing was rapid and his face was glistening with beads of sweat. They recounted the night's events quickly.

"Well lad, I think this is not the place to hide! They know well my association with thee now."

Tom nodded.

"But we had nowhere else to go… and we had to protect the chalice…"

"How can thou…"

The words were obscured by a sudden noise from the passage. The door had flung open and the familiar scratching noises echoed around the slate flag floor.

Everyone froze and James had a horrified expression on his face. He was not in any fit state to run further.

Jackson and Tom raced to the door to bar it with the oak settle. As they reached it to close it firmly a scrawny arm and claw like hands pushed through the gap. They heaved with all their might and shoved the heavy door shut. The arm shattered like glass and shards of sandstone fell to the floor. An unearthly scream pierced the night like a dagger. Rob shuddered. The creatures clamoured at the door and rattled the lock. He rushed to add his weight, as did James. They managed to wedge the heavy settle that they had dragged across the room, against the door. The door creaked and bulged with the supernatural strength of the evil creatures. Tom pushed his weight against it and called to Jackson to show them the trap door. He lifted the door with the metal ring and pushed James and Rob into the disused cockpit. He handed down a candle and then told them how to exit through the concealed doorway. Rob hesitated and looked back at Tom wistfully... how would he manage to stave off the attack with only the old man?

"Go Rob! Just get thee gone!" he cried anticipating Rob's protests. "Get thee away... 'twill be dawn soon enough and these devils will lose their magic with the rising sun! Go..."

"I..." no words would come. Rob knew that he would probably not see him again... at least not in this life.

Tom smiled and then turned his attention back to the door. Jackson grinned and shut the trap door. They could hear furniture moving – it sounded as though something heavy had been dragged over the trap door.

James hurried him along and they entered the secret

passage which led them back out to the coast. It was dark and the wind, which blew from the entrance, caught the candle flame and extinguished it.

"That's all we need!" exploded Rob.

"Keep on… I believe I can see light ahead… we must be close to entrance."

Sure enough they emerged onto the banking above the beach. Rob understood how useful this tunnel must have been to the smugglers. They emerged into the pale yellow and pink light of dawn. The insipid colours were growing in strength and a liquid golden sun emerged above the horizon. Both James and Rob breathed a great sigh of relief as they realised that the creatures would now expire. On cue they heard a dreadful blood curdling howl from the gargoyles back at the inn. At least they knew that Tom and Jackson would be safe now.

They turned to find their way back and saw to their horror that Silas Dixon was emerging from the tunnel. He faced them with an animal like roar.

"Give back that which is mine!"

James threw the package to Rob who caught it deftly.

"Run Rob… I will hold this devil while you make good your escape!"

Rob looked doubtful. He was concerned for James… how could he fight off Dixon who was built like one of his solid barns.

"Go I say! I shall endure!"

Rob turned and ran. He looked behind him to find the first mayor of Barrow grappling with Dixon like a

'WWF wrestler'! Just went to show, you really should not judge a book by its cover.

He ran and ran. He was not sure where he was going, but as he got further from Silas he became more positive. He looked back again. This time the two figures were obscured by a vortex of dust and sand. He watched in slow motion as the vortex moved relentlessly towards him. All sense left him and he floated in his dream state, hearing distant voices and seeing vivid images pass before him. He clung to the chalice for dear life, the only thing tangible and real. In the distance he could see a room. It was one he was unfamiliar with.

The room sharpened and became clear, just like when you adjusted the settings on the television. He could see a familiar figure laying on a bed, beside him a concerned young woman. It was George. His face was colourless and he had dark rings around his eyes. He was thin and wasted and unconscious. His mother's face was drawn and weary and Rob wondered how many days she had been nursing him in this way.

The boy in the bed stirred. He was fitful and feverish. His mother wiped his forehead with a cool flannel and spoke soft words to him. Suddenly, he sat bolt upright and pointed at him. Rob jumped. He had not expected to be seen. George's mother looked to where he was pointing puzzled.

"George, what's wrong? There's nobody there…"

"Creatures… beware … the creatures…" he panted.

Rob smiled and said quietly, "There are no creatures… we have beaten them!"

"No! They'll stop you… watch out!" he was very agitated.

His mother looked again and for a fleeting moment Rob almost believed she could see him too. Their eyes connected. Her brilliant blue eyes damp with tears of concern. He wanted to call out to her and tell her it would be alright.

George fell back on his pillow and drifted into a deep sleep again.

Rob was overcome with giddiness and nausea again as he drifted on through time itself. He arrived at his destination with a thud. He was in Abbot's Wood once more. There was no sign of James or his magnificent Victorian villa. He hoped for a second that he had arrived home. It became rapidly apparent that he was not 'home'. Instead the wood was darker, denser and untamed. The silence in the wood was deafening and uncanny. The birds were silent and there was hardly a breath of wind. The sun was setting – his body clock told him this was wrong… he had just left the dawn at Rampside and goodness knew what time it had been in George's house. He was totally disorientated. Something was amiss. He could hear no birds and usually at this time of day the birdsong was heard clearly. Malevolence had encased the woods; dark shadows pervaded the hollows and nooks within the trees and the night sky seeped like black ink blotting out the horizon. Within minutes it was as dark as a raven's wing. An insipid crescent moon rose, shedding little light and tiny pinpricks of white light spattered the velvet sky like droplets of paint.

Rob pushed the chalice deeper into his pocket unconsciously attempting to hide it. Evil cast its heavy shadow around, invisible grasping fingers of darkness reaching for the bright treasure. He shivered as unseen eyes bored into his flesh like needles. He looked around like a fugitive, afraid of who or what he would see. He knew he was vulnerable in the open and he followed a well-worn path into the trees away from the clearing he had landed in. He could make no sense of his location, there were no landmarks that he recognised and even if he could see some, the darkness would have obscured them. He stumbled about in the undergrowth and wandered down the tree-covered hillside. He stopped at the bottom and tried to find his bearings.

A plaintive tune drifted from across the valley. The plain song was sweet and melodic, mournful and beautiful. This truly was music to his ears. He recognised it immediately as the Gregorian chants the monks made with only the human voice as an instrument. The hairs stood up on the back of his neck and he realised few people from his century would have ever heard such a pure and exquisite sound other than on recordings. He paused for a while drinking in the sound. Rob followed the direction the music was coming from, guessing that he would find some level of safety if he went to the abbey. As he stumbled closer and the trees thinned out he could see the shadowy shape of the abbey rising ahead of him. Pale lights flickered from behind windows, which rose into magnificent arches pointing their way to heaven. He was encouraged and staggered onwards over twisted roots and discarded logs. He reached an open meadow and the abbey revealed itself in its grandeur. The visitors' lodge and Lady Chapel lay ahead, this building he did recognise and he made his way towards it. Unexpectedly, a figure bowled out of the shadows, running erratically towards him. A second followed and then a third. The first crashed headlong into him knocking him over.

Rob was winded and the chalice shot into the air revealing its gleaming beauty. It fell from its coverings and was visible, the gold and copper alloy glinting in the meagre moonlight. A gasp arose from the person who lay sprawled on the floor. The other two figures ran to his aid and the older one reached for the cup. Rob was quicker and caught the object deftly, wrapping it quickly and pushing it into his pocket.

"What treasure dost thou conceal lad? Cannot be thine… thou must have stolen it form the church!"

Rob looked at the man. He was dressed in a long white robe like John Stell but his face belied his evil ways. His eyes narrowed and his thin features were as immobile as the statues around the abbey walls. The other monks approached, imbued with courage from their brother's challenge to the boy. They circled Rob like hyenas and his heart banged liked a hammer. These monks were of a different mettle than John Stell. They closed in on the boy and the elder monk – the one who appeared to be their leader drew a sharp knife from his leather bag on his girdle. It was obvious that this man would stop at nothing to acquire the golden object he had seen. Rob had the impression that he had already taken a life and that his would be no more to him than swatting a fly. Before the three could conclude their encounter he dodged between them and ran for his life. The adrenalin raced through every vein and he discovered how fast he could run, faster than he had ever run during a football match. He ran like the wind and sprinted past the abbey where services were still going on. The monks pursued him hotly and were determined to catch him and claim their prize. Rob ran through more trees and up a hillside faster than a mountain goat and just as fleet footed. As he reached the summit he suddenly realised where he was.

He was at the old quarry where the trouble had begun, where Nate had become strange and ill. The place was just as odd as it had been the last time he had visited it. An invisible energy hummed and buzzed. He touched his forehead to rub away the fuzzy headache he seemed to have acquired. The trees rustled and the monks broke through surrounding him once more. Rob was alarmed. He could see no way out this time. The sides of the hill were too steep to run down and he did not know where to go next. The elder monk wrested the chalice from his pocket, grabbing it so viciously that the jacket ripped. Just as he thought all was lost the hum of energy grew louder and was so brittle that it made his ears hurt. He gaped as the chalice fell from the monk's hand. He grasped it as if it had burnt him and yelped with pain. The other two sprang back in fear.

The monk sank to his knees, pushed down by some invisible force. He grabbed hold of one of the sandstone rocks protruding from the ground and as he did so his face contorted into a horrible mask. He became one with the rock and with a terrible scream he was absorbed into it forever. The grimace was frozen and his moment of defeat recorded for all time. The other two blanched and began to run, but the supernatural power, which had vanquished their brother, claimed them too. Their demise was no less horrifying than his. Every cell was congealed and their blood, bones and sinews were solidified into the unyielding rock. The pain of their punishment was etched on their faces, which would be frozen for eternity, a testament of their treachery. The abbot's blood was on their hands and the chalice had reminded them and caused them to be interred forever, imprisoned in stone but still aware. They would have centuries to contemplate their deeds… and their fate.

A bright light enveloped Rob and he floated like a feather, drifting on the waves of time, which encircled him like a protective mother's arms. He could hear the chants from the abbey, flowing over him like ripples of water…

Procedamus in pace…

The crystal clear voices rose and fell in a language he

did not understand, but the lyrical rich sound of the Latin words soothed him.

In nomine Christi, Amen
Cum angelis et pueris,

The perfect sound hovered just within his consciousness. He felt tired and he closed his eyes. He wondered if this was what dying felt like. Drifting on a cloud of nothingness and fading away to the sound of inspiring music. He was more completely relaxed than he had been since this adventure had begun...

fideles inveniamur
Drifting aimlessly... no cares
Procedamus in pace
In nomine Christi, Amen ...
Let us proceed in peace, in the name of Christ Amen

CHAPTER 21

BACK TO NORMAL

Rob awoke and prised open his heavy eyelids apprehensively. He was drained of energy and was astounded to find he was in his own room, in bed. He looked down at his T-shirt... the one he had worn the night before the adventure. How long had he been away? How had he returned? So many questions and very few answers. He rubbed his eyes and had almost convinced himself he had dreamed it all when he spotted his jeans and Doc Marten's. They were covered in dried mud and much of it had crumbled and fallen onto the carpet. He jumped when he remembered they had rescued the chalice... where was it? He leapt from his bed and rooted through the clothes he had dumped in a pile on the floor. Relief rushed over him as he found it, still wrapped in its coverings. He pulled it from the jacket and noticed the big tear in the pocket. So he had not imagined the events of yesterday... yesterday? It seemed much longer and he had seen too many dawns and sunsets to have only been away one day.

He scrambled to hide the chalice in the trunk beneath his window. He buried it beneath his prized possessions; nobody would know where it was... he hoped. He emerged from the bedroom looking as if he had been forcibly dragged through a hedge backwards. He wandered along the landing to see how his brother and sister were. Remarkably they were just stirring. He peered into Rebecca's room. The girl was sitting up in bed; her hair tangled and knotted, but her cheeks a healthy pink again.

"You ok now?" he said gruffly.

She nodded slowly as if she was checking whether she did feel ok.

"Yeah... but I had some weird dreams... all about you looking for the chalice... and monks... and strange people from centuries ago... and those scary gargoyle things!" She shuddered at the memory.

He smiled. Somehow she must have seen what he had been through. It certainly seemed like a dream to him now.

"Well as long as you feel better... you had us worried," he added.

Nate came out of his room and bounced across Rebecca's bed. Evidently he was much better too. Rob was relieved.

"What are you two doin' haven't we got some work to do? You know..." he dropped his voice to a whisper, "the chalice... we have to find it!"

Rob laughed out loud.

"It's not funny... we need to find it before something bad happens."

"Too late for that! Bad things have happened... not that you two sleeping beauties were any use!"

"What do you mean?" asked Rebecca.

He related the strange tale and both of them stared incredulously at him.

"That is a bit spooky," said Nate, "I was dreaming all night last night and I kept seeing Tom and Dolly and you… and Silas… oh and George… but he was out for the count –he was ill…"

"I don't think it was a dream. I think it was for real and you two somehow were able to witness it."

"How come?" asked Nate.

"I dunno… but maybe because we're family? And we are all connected to these treasures. Don't you remember being ill? Both of you were so fast asleep I thought you'd never wake up… and if I hadn't found the chalice I don't think you would have done. We must take care to return it to the abbey, John Stell must have it, but how we will get there unseen I don't know. One thing I do know, we mustn't go near the old quarry – there's something magic about that place and those monks are still up there, waiting to be freed. Well, I for one don't want to be anywhere near if they get their wish…"

Chapter 22

Diversion

They put their worries behind them and raced downstairs to have breakfast. Nothing could be achieved on an empty stomach – so Nate said. They were all feeling more positive about this final task, after all they had vanquished the dark ones so many times, this could not be too difficult. Even so, Rob was nervous and insisted on checking on the chalice every few minutes, even though they had not left the house.

"We have to think of a way to return the chalice without being noticed. I'm sure if we reach the abbey safely we will be able to summon John Stell," said Nate.

"But how will we get there? Those horrible magpies are perched everywhere," remarked Rebecca. She had been watching them land silently, one by one on branches and fences around the house.

"Hmm. That's a point. They do seem to be able to contact Silas… even in the eighteenth century added Rob ruefully.

They fell quiet and retreated into their own thoughts. It was a knotty problem. They decided that whatever happened, the chalice must not be left alone again. It must be carried with them. Rob suggested they stuck together, "after all they say there's safety in numbers!"

"I know!" yelled Nate, "What if we each take a bag, they wouldn't know who had the chalice and if we are split up we have more chance of fooling them! You know, like a decoy!" He was quite excited at the thought.

They each took a back-pack. Rob wrapped the chalice carefully in a towel and pushed it into his. Nate found a vase of a similar size and did the same, while Rebecca wrapped up a brass candlestick and placed it into her bag. They were satisfied that their ruse would work, or at least buy them time. The only other problem to solve was how to reach the abbey without being followed or stopped. By chance Dad was going to town and Rob suggested they hitch a lift.

"But town's miles from the abbey, we'll have to walk!" moaned Rebecca.

"Look we don't want them to think we're going to the abbey, do we? We have to pretend and distract them," explained Rob.

"Ok but I don't know how it's gonna work…"

"Well, it's our only chance, we have to try!" said Nate.

They told Dad they were going to the pictures. He was happy to drop them off at the Apollo cinema at Hollywood Park. They watched as he left and walked towards the cinema. The plan was for them to go to the cinema and then for Rob, to slip out and make his way to the abbey on foot or by taxi. Hopefully, they would not be detected, but it was not a totally convincing plan.

They had to make it look convincing and spent a lot of time arguing about which film to see. They bought popcorn and a drink and made their way to Screen Two. The theatre was fairly empty, so they were able to choose their seats. While they were waiting for the lights to go down Rob nudged them to listen.

"When the film starts I'll nip down the stairs and go to the emergency exit. But you'll have to stay till the end of the film!" he whispered.

"Too right we will," said Nate stretching his legs carelessly over the empty seat in front. "I'm not paying for a film and then missing it."

Rob raised his eyebrows. Rebecca giggled.

"Well at least it's a decent film... *Nanny McPhee*!" she said, "It's only been out since January!"

"Huh! So *you* say!" retorted Nate.

"Never mind the film! This is to put them off the scent! But keep your eyes open – you don't know who's around... and if anyone follows me you'll have to distract them or something. You've got your bags if we take three different directions they won't know who to follow."

Nate chuckled, "It's not an episode of *Spooks* y'know," referring to Rob's favourite TV programme about spies.

"It feels like it is. I don't trust anyone now. Look!" he nodded towards an elderly lady eating ice cream, "She could be one of them."

The old lady, rosy cheeked, plump and unconcerned did not look suspicious to Nate. He snorted contemptuously. He was used to his brother's sense of drama.

The film got into full swing and was quite noisy. As

soon as the audience was absorbed he slipped quickly down the steps and through the Emergency exit as he had planned. The adrenalin was racing through is veins and he smirked to himself as he began humming the theme tune to *Spooks*; at least it released the tension.

He emerged from the rear of the cinema and looked carefully before he ran towards the town. He ran through back streets and changed direction frequently, pausing now and then in doorways to check there were no magpies or other acolytes of Silas Dixon following him. He dodged the traffic on Abbey Road and sped into the park. He wanted to avoid a direct route and this would take him towards Newbarns and then he could double back to the abbey. He ran along the path, which led to the Cenotaph on top of the hill. It was a sacred place commemorating the dead from two World Wars. He had always been fascinated with it and had watched the Remembrance parades and even taken part in some as a boy scout.

The air ahead was hazy, like in a heat wave, but today was not warm. He knew what was about to happen and instead of trying to avoid it he let the temporal waves wash over him gently. He witnessed the Cenotaph disappear and the park receded. In its place was a barren grass covered hill. It was a massive earthwork, with ditches and ramparts. Stationed around were fierce looking tribesmen, wild and rugged, daubed with blue paint. They carried primitive spears and others herded cattle towards the pasture below. Smoke from wood fires rose from the enclosure and he could see squat round houses scattered around the base of the fortification. The park to the east was covered with trees as far as the eye could see and the countryside was as yet wild and untamed, with only small incursions from agriculture. He could only guess 'when' he was, but he had read somewhere that there had been an Iron Age settlement and hill fort at the site of the park. It looked primitive enough to be the 'Black Castle' of legend. He was rooted to the spot, unsure why he had been taken so far back in time. He was terrified the tribesmen would see him, they were fierce and he would not care to risk bumping into them.

He moved stealthily into the trees and tried to gain his bearings, his pulse was racing. He would have to attempt to travel to the location of the abbey. If this time frame continued he would have no real points of reference. Even the abbey would not yet be built. It was strange; a great power surged through the trees almost knocking him from his feet. Time was out of control; there were no constraints or boundaries any longer. He wondered if the recent events had fractured the natural order and this was why he was ricocheting through different ages. The atmosphere wobbled and shook again; he witnessed colours, shapes and mysterious ghostly figures pass before his eyes. It was a surreal parade, intangible and ethereal. If you could 'fast forward' history this is what it would be like, he thought.

When the movement finally ceased he was amongst a crowd of people. Much to his relief he had been brought forward in time to more familiar surroundings. He was still in the Park and he could see a Cenotaph rising ahead, draped in two Union Jack flags. Military bands were playing and men, women and children stood respectfully as the mayor, Walker Fairbairn spoke. The time was the early twentieth century judging by the clothes and uniforms people wore.

Rob knew exactly where he was now. It had to be Armistice Day, 11 November. The year was 1921 when Barrow officially mourned and honoured their war dead of the Great War. He had read about this in history and was interested in this period. He had discovered information about his great, great uncles who had perished in the conflict and he was overawed to be witnessing such a moving episode in the town's history. He knew that everyone around him would have known someone lost in the terrible war.

The sound of a buzzer split the silence... just as it had a Granddad's funeral, a chill ran down his spine. This was followed by the loud boom of a field gun from the front; rolling like thunder and making the air around them vibrate. Silence prevailed at the eleventh hour and Field Marshal Sir William Robertson pressed a lever, which cut the cords attached to the flags. They fell smoothly to the ground revealing the pure white obelisk, piercing the blue sky and gleaming in the brilliant sunshine. A gasp went up from the crowd and people stared, some dabbing eyes with handkerchiefs, others choking back the tears and many straining to see their loved one's name inscribed on the panels around the memorial. The Bishop of Carlisle presided over prayers and expressed a collective gratitude for the ultimate sacrifice that the men of the town had made.

Rob stood stock-still. He felt tears prickling his eyes and began to understand the enormity of the loss to the town of over six hundred men. He shivered with emotion and realised how dreadful an impact this war must have had, not just on his own little town, but on the rest of the country too.

A hand grabbed his sleeve and tugged at it. He looked around and saw a young man, dressed in a railway man's uniform. He looked strangely familiar. He was short and stocky, with a straight nose and clear blue eyes, which saw into his very soul. His sand coloured hair was already receding and was swept off his forehead. He smiled, eyes twinkling and spoke with a broad Cumberland accent.

"Tha needs t' folla me lad! Yon li'le fella over there towld me that thou needs a lift up t' abbey!" He pointed with his thumb over his shoulder. He caught sight of a scrawny kid in cap and clogs with rather large ears. It was George… but he faded as he watched and vanished without trace. Suddenly, Rob knew who he was speaking to. It was George's father. Obviously, he had no knowledge of who the boy was. He had not been born yet. This grew stranger by the minute. George must still be trapped in his dream state… he must still be ill. Rob had assumed that he too would be released from the illness as his own brother and sister had been.

He looked at the young man – his own great-grandfather. He was going to be more familiar with his ancestors than his immediate family at this rate!

"C'mon then, we 'avn't got all day! Get crackin'! Oh and I'm Ben by the way" As he walked away he lit his pipe and Rob followed the smell of the tobacco through the crowd. They walked down the hill to Abbey Road where Ben had left his horse and delivery wagon. He got up and beckoned Rob to join him. They set off with a jolt, but the ride was smoother than with John Jackson, at least this road was less pitted and better made. They trundled along the tree-lined road, it was less busy than in his own time, but had the addition of trams instead of cars zooming up and down. Rob turned around to see one as it rattled past.

"Hast tha not seen one of those afore lad?" Ben chuckled. "Is tha from up country?"

Rob grinned and nodded.

"'Was a moving service up at yon cenotaph right enough!" Ben continued, "I lost two brothers on the Somme so it's nice t' see all the lads who died remembered."

Ben fell silent, lost in his own thoughts. He sucked on the pipe steadily and as they reached Manor Farm Rob began to feel apprehensive. He looked anxiously around him and was relieved not to see any magpies around. Ben noticed his nervousness and the fact that he jumped at every loud noise. They stopped near the old cottage, just as Jackson had done. Rob was having a real déjà vu sensation… but at least he knew that it was not just his imagination. He expected to see a magpie or two, but there were none. He got down from the delivery cart and turned to see Ben doing the same.

"Er thanks for the lift Ben…"

"I'll be with thee fer a bit… ya seem all of a jitter," he re-lit the pipe, "I have an idea tha might need help?"

He examined Rob closely staring straight at him.

"That's ok… honest!"

"Nay, I said I'd tag along… where ya headed?" he asked.

Silence. Where indeed? He hadn't a clue where to start. Everywhere seemed sterile and peaceful. Perhaps this was a good thing. There was no indication of anyone watching them, but he was uncomfortable somehow and was secretly pleased that Ben was staying.

"Er… I have to return something, but I have to find the right person."

Ben nodded impassively. He took off his jacket and laid it on the seat, he presented a formidable figure. Powerfully built he reminded Rob of a thick-set terrier they had once had. He suddenly felt safer; it would be a brave man who would confront this young man. Rob realised that he had probably seen more conflict and danger than he would ever see. He wondered how tough this man must be to survive the trenches and to come home and take up a normal life. Many failed – he knew, but somehow Ben had inner steel and was evidently a fighter.

They walked towards the abbey and approached the gate. A surprise greeted him. Mr Mason was there, dressed smartly in his Ministry of Works uniform and cap. He winked at him as they approached. Rob wasn't sure if this meant he knew him from the future or was just being friendly. Rebecca had told him that Mason was from George's time and could move between the different timelines-so it was hard to tell.

"Alright Ben?"

"Aye not bad Robert, we just want a little wander if that's alright?"

The two men knew each other.

"How's the missus? How's your lad? When was he born?" asked Mason.

"July. He's champion! We called him Bill after our kid…" Ben's face crumpled a little at the memory of his brother.

Rob pricked his ears up. He reckoned that the baby must be George's older brother. George was not due to arrive for another two years. How surprised Ben would be if he knew that another son and two daughters would follow at regular two-year intervals. He yearned to tell him who he really was. Mason pre-empted any attempt he might make by sending them on their way.

They wandered aimlessly around the abbey. Rob hoped that the monk would make an appearance. There must be some way to summon him. They walked across the cloister and towards the Chapter House. This was a significant place and had been where the sword had been claimed. They walked through the arch and there was nothing. No crackling energy, no feeling of dizziness… nothing! It was very disappointing and frustrating.

"So who is it tha's looking for lad?" asked Ben.

"Er…"

"Go on…"

"Er… a monk," he was almost embarrassed to admit to it.

"John Stell tha means?"

Rob tripped over his own feet he was so shocked.

"You know?"

"Course I do! It's a family thing," he laughed. "Way back we have summat t' do with the family he came from… and we're all part of the Brotherhood, y'know to protect the abbey and its treasures."

"I wish you'd said…"

"I have… now!" he laughed again, "Well we'd better get crackin'."

He strode off towards the abbot's house. Rob ran to keep up and as they reached the building. Ben disappeared through the remnants of a doorway and disappeared out of sight. He followed and caught sight of him vanishing into the tunnel, which ran beneath the abbot's lodgings. He crouched down and followed him through the low passage. It wasn't very long and they could see the other end easily. Rob wondered what the point was of travelling through such a small tunnel and then he remembered that this was the way he had originally entered James Ramsden's time.

They emerged at the other end and immediately Rob could see immediately that they had found their way back to earlier times. The abbey was fully built, new and bright, the sandstone radiated a warm pink colour, which in the twenty-first century was obscured by lichens and damaged by acid rain and pollution. The bright sunlight enhanced the building and the carvings were sharp and as clear as the day they had been made. The stained glass windows caught the light and sparkled like a million prisms, refracting light beams into tiny rainbows that played across the grass. Ben continued on, undeterred by the current state of the building. As they approached the door into the transept they could hear the pure voices of the Quire monks. There was a service, judging by the time of day it was Nones the afternoon office. Ben concealed himself behind one of the huge pillars along from the presbytery. Rob followed suit. The service was over and the monks dispersed to the refectory to have their ale, to refresh them before their work. Ben slipped into the church and past the choir stalls. They walked into the cloister, which was empty.

Rob gasped. The cloister was an enclosed quadrangle, with a covered walkway. Here and there were small writing desks and wooden stools, the floors were covered with green glazed tiles, which reflected the light. On the north side light flooded in providing excellent working conditions for the abbey scribes. The cloister was used in summer as a scriptorium but in winter they retreated to the undercroft, beneath the dormitory. He and Ben stood in the shadows beside a huge cupboard, fashioned from one of the Norman arches along the east wall. A large wooden door was ajar, revealing shelves holding parchment, books, inks and goose feather quills. Rob was fascinated and had often wondered what the strange arches had held. Soon an elderly monk came along the cloister range towards them. It was John Stell.

He knew they were waiting. He led them to his writing slope and sat down. He looked weary and older than Rob had remembered. He smiled at them and nodded.

"Welcome both, ye are most welcome. I have been expecting you."

Ben nodded and returned the smile.

"You have brought the chalice I trust?"

This time it was Rob who nodded. He began to remove the back sack from his shoulders. The monk lifted a hand to stop him.

"Nay, we must wait," he shook his head sorrowfully. "We can only safeguard this treasure when none can witness it. Ye are both still in peril and thy futures... and past depend upon us reversing the evil which has been wrought by Silas Dixon in thy time Robert."

Rob was startled at hearing his full name. He opened his mouth to speak but the monk continued.

"Damage has been done which can only be repaired in time... and by time. The chalice has been used for ill and we must pay the penance. I sense a great evil brewing which will affect thee and thine across the years. We can limit this damage if we can conceal the chalice forever."

"How do we do that Brother?" asked Ben.

"We wait until the appointed time... and we must conceal thee till then. Follow me and be silent and reverent."

The two of them followed the monk, who led them outside. The abbey was quiet and deserted; the monks were now engaged in their daily tasks. They walked towards the infirmary. It was dark and silent, empty apart from an elderly monk who was being cared for in one of the cells along the long room. They left the building unseen and walked towards a number of scattered buildings in what was the amphitheatre. The

Custodian's cottage, which Rob had seen in various states was a large building, taller and more imposing. They walked past this onto a small workshop, surrounded by a luxuriant but tightly packed herb garden. They entered the wooden building; it was dark and musty inside. They could smell the faint aroma of herbs and potions and beams of light shone through the ill-fitting slats on the wooden shutter revealing the dust particles hanging in the air. The room had a workbench and stools, a fire and the floor was strewn with sweet smelling rushes. It was practical but there was not much comfort to be had.

Stell beckoned them to sit and they obeyed. There was little else to do. He instructed them to stay until he returned at nightfall. When he had gone they whispered to each other. It was going to be a long few hours. The hut, for that's all it really was, was stifling and dry. Rob sneezed and coughed, irritated by the pollen and dust.

Later in the afternoon Brother John had brought a small draught of ale in an earthenware jug and two wooden beakers. The slight meal he provided consisted of a couple of raw onions, a piece of suspect looking cheese and even rougher bread than he had sampled at Tom's house. Neither he nor Ben were very enthusiastic about the food and tried the ale instead. It was unlike any beer they had tasted. It was weak and a bit tasteless, but at least it was liquid and it served to quench their thirst. The sun beat down on the little hut and it became airless and stuffy. They grew drowsy, dozing and talking in intervals.

A couple of times they heard voices outside and

anxiously looked around for a place to hide. Luckily nobody came in and they were not presented with the problem of hiding. Eventually, the hut cooled down and dusk drew in. They risked eating the simple food John Stell had provided and finished off the ale. They were beginning to think that they would never see the monk again, when the door opened. Cool night air rushed into the small room. The monk carried a swill basket full of lavender, which he put down on the wooden bench.

"I used this subterfuge in case I was seen," he explained, "We must move speedily if we are to install the chalice safely."

They stood up and stretched, their aching limbs glad to move at last. They followed Stell into the darkness outside. The cooler air was refreshing and they welcomed it. The stars stapled the black cloudless sky like a spangled cloak. The wild garlic smelt pungent and quiet surrounded the precinct, disturbed now and then by a distant hoot or night call. They followed the spritely monk back into the abbey. It was silent and dark apart from a solitary rush light at the cloister door. Stell was like a mole, he was just as confident finding his way in the darkness as he was in the light. The monks were in bed, retiring early in the summer, because their first services were at 2.30 a.m. Stell had used this opportunity to bring them into the abbey unseen.

They entered the undercroft quietly. It was deserted and the room echoed with their footfalls. Evidence of the work of the day was left unfinished on the trestle tables, shoes being mended, clothes to stitch and all number of everyday tasks. It was cold and dark, the fire unlit and no rush lights. They could make out the figure of Stell from the fraction of light, which broke through the windows; he made his way to the huge fireplace in the middle of the wall, half way down the room.

"I have a safe place prepared for the chalice. It will be protected here, God willing," he whispered.

He knelt at the base of the hearth and pressed a carved tile. The tile had a carving, not of a sprig of nightshade this time, instead the simple shape of a decorative cross.

"X marks the spot eh, brother?" smirked Ben.

The tile slid back and revealed a deep cut hole. He took the chalice offered by Rob, carefully bound it in the wrappings and gently laid it in the gap. The tile slid back and the treasure was concealed once more.

The three left the room and slowly walked to the tunnel entrance behind the abbey.

"How do we know it will be safe? How do we know it won't be found again?" asked Rob.

"We must pray and hope it is not found. We can only do so much to protect it and evil has been done already. Each time the chalice is ill used, it weakens in its power."

The thought was sobering. The monk smiled. Dawn was rising and melting away the night. The birds heralded its appearance and the bell rang for Lauds.

"We must say our farewells, ye will see me more, but for now thou must depart. God bless thee my sons."

Ben and Rob shuffled through the tunnel in silence. They had returned to Ben's time, which was at least slightly safer than Rob's. The mood was subdued as they made their way back through the gate to the cart. Mason nodded and raised a quizzical eyebrow as they passed and Ben acknowledged with a slight wave.

"So lad, what's your plan now?"

"Dunno… got to get back home…"

"Aye it's a bit of a pain till tha gets used to it… you'll be back right enough, it always happens when you least expect it." Ben spoke with authority.

"So has this always happened to you… moving through time, seeing the monk and everything?"

"Aye. As long as I can remember. When I was a lad at Ravenglass I used to see the owld monk but he never spoke. I reckon it's a gift some of us have and some of us don't."

They travelled back towards the town. It was quiet and was growing dark. It took some getting used to – starting out in one season and ending up in another, all in a few hours. It was like a weird sort of jet lag… and you always seemed to have the wrong clothes on. It was still November in this time and he was not as warmly dressed as he would have liked. They trundled on down to the Strand, a commercial road, which led to the original heart of Barrow village. He wondered where they were going until Ben drove the horse into a yard through a brick built arch. He jumped down and unhitched the horse to take him into the railway stable. Rob followed and watched him gently tend to the needs of the old nag. Once fed and watered Ben rubbed the horse down. Rob was touched by the man's tenderness and his heart swelled with pride. Something of his inner nature shone through and Rob was pleased to have met him. He was wondering what he would say if he told him who he was… it surely couldn't harm. As though he could read his thoughts Ben glanced at him, his blue eyes fixing on him. A shiver went through Rob as he suddenly recognised how like George he was… and of course George – well, he was in no doubt now as to his true identity. Drowsiness made his eyelids heavy and he yawned.

He was overcome by an intense need to sleep and though he fought it he could not keep his eyes from closing. He fell into a deep slumber, cushioned by his dreams and away from harm.

"Did ya do it then?"

"Wake up! What ya doin' in bed?"

He shook himself awake and found his brother and sister leaning over him. He was fully clothed but was beneath his duvet. He was startled to find himself back home, let alone in bed.

"Did you? Did you do it? The chalice? Is it safe?" demanded Rebecca impatiently.

"Er…yeah! I think so…" he said vaguely.

His head spun with cluttered memories and thoughts.

His siblings looked eagerly for his response, hoping he would elaborate. He briefly told them what had happened and as he spoke he did not feel confident that the solution was the best.

"So it's back in the abbey? But is it safe there? Why didn't John Stell take it to the same place the sword went to?" asked Nate.

"Well the sacred book is in a museum, so maybe it

doesn't matter where it is once it's been taken from the bad ones!" Rebecca offered.

"I don't know, but he seemed to be happy that it was in the abbey again... I was a bit worried though... because how does he know it will survive until now?"

"Only one way to find out..."

"Anyone else feel like we are going round in circles?" Nate sighed. "It's like a game of hide and seek – through time.

Chapter 23

Saving the Future

Something strange had happened, nothing felt right. They were gripped by a sense of inertia. Rob fell into a malaise and became quiet and withdrawn. He could not even muster the energy to tease his brother. Rebecca was irritating everyone with her incessant chatter and questions, none of which either boy could answer. Nate was grumpy and he retreated into a TV world of science fiction and vampires. The days were growing warmer and although the weather was fine none of them left the house except to go to school and work.

Rob frequently caught himself looking at his great granddad's photo. It was Ben alright, but in uniform seated on a big black horse, wielding a lance and sporting a heavy moustache. He stared at it intently, hoping he would find answers. He even found pictures of George and looked at every aspect closely, trying to find clues or something they had overlooked. Nothing revealed itself to him.

They went about their business, but didn't go near the abbey. Each one of them watched for birds or strange creatures, but nothing seemed to be unusual. The lone raven nested nearby and gave them some solace. He was their sentry and protector, or so they hoped. The odd thing was they didn't want to discuss the situation either. Rob began to despair as to whether they would discover if their efforts had been successful.

Rob was struggling to sleep again, as he had for many nights since his last adventure. The strange experiences he and his brother and sister had been through re-ran in his brain like an old movie. He analysed the final meeting with John Stell and Ben over and over, but could find no peace. The night was close and airless and a full moon shone into his room producing an unsettling effect. The room was bathed in silvery light, leeching the colour and definition from everything, the dark corners hiding unknown secrets. He looked around nervously. Suddenly, he was reduced to childish fears of the dark and monsters under the bed. He argued with himself not to be so silly, reasoning that after the amazing things he had seen, he should be fearless.

His eyes were itching with tiredness and he ached for sleep. As he fought with insomnia a tiny blue crackle burst in the darkest corner of the room. His eyes opened wider and he held his breath.

Crackle… crackle…

A larger burst of energy fractured the darkness. Blue light spat and sputtered like a roman candle, gaining size and intensity. From within its centre a familiar figure emerged.

The boy looked pale and ill. It was George. He was gaunt and thin. He was ill. He smiled weakly and waved.

"George?"

"I'm ill…"

"What can I do?"

"I haven't long… you have to help… the chalice is still in danger."

Rob caught his breath. His heart sank and he felt sick.

"But it's at the abbey."

"But they are looking; they want the rest of its power… I can't get better while it's in danger… and I can't help you."

"What do we have to do George?"

"Get it before they find it… if they use it again our lives are forfeit… they will change the passage of time forever."

Rob was silent.

"But where will we take it? How can we save it?"

"Others will help you, find Mason, he is waiting… but don't…"

His voice dimmed, as did the light surrounding him.

"Don't what?"

The boy tried to make himself heard, but faded gradually. His strength was waning. He reached out to Rob but it was too late the magic was trickling away. The light snapped off leaving dark silence.

Rob determined to return to the abbey and retrieve the chalice. It was like a game of cat and mouse, but it was impossible to know who was actually winning. The others would have to be told and the mission was on again. He felt better than he had for weeks, at least there was some movement and they might be able to settle things for once and for all. The treasure was safe for now, but they would need to move quickly before Dixon and his cohorts had the chance to discover where it lay. He sensed a change in the atmosphere. This was more important and more dangerous than any of their other adventures.

CHAPTER 24

AWAKENINGS

Fingers of bright moonlight picked their way across the sleeping stones of the Chapter House and rested upon a crude carving inscribed into the wall. The light etched the features of a face, a face frozen in fear, its mouth forever open in a petrified scream. The eyes were holes bored deep and fathomless into the stone conveying a desolate horror. Dixon emerged from the shadows and drew parallel with the small carving. He craned his neck so to see the face more clearly and he tentatively reached up with a black-gloved hand. He covered the face with his claw like fingers, obscuring it from view.

An owl screeched, signalling an alarm throughout Abbot's Wood, the night creatures heard it and crept away quietly into the undergrowth, camouflaging and removing themselves from sight. There was a hum of energy emitting from the abbey and the very stones vibrated ominously. Dixon became as inert as the walls and his black silhouette increased in density. The tension and silence met in an uncomfortable union and great power flowed from Dixon's hand into the wall. The sandstone shifted and shimmered with an electrical current, bringing vibrancy and life to the masonry. A purple glow held the stones and grew in brightness until man and wall became one. An enormous surge of power cracked and echoed through the Chapter House and Dixon was flung backwards onto the ground. The wall throbbed and pulsed hypnotically and the low hum resonated threateningly. The face shifted and contorted, mouth and eyes moving manically as they emerged from the stone.

The head pulled away from its rigid prison, flashes of amethyst light sparked and flashed as the head forced its way out, shoulders following. Arms pushed and struggled to attain freedom, finally followed by torso and legs, an unnatural birthing of a resurrected, unholy soul.

The creature landed heavily at Dixon's feet and he bent to raise him up. The figure was emaciated and crooked from his long sojourn encased within the sandstone. He winced as he stretched and uncurled, every bone and sinew creaking and snapping into place. With superhuman effort he stretched and resumed his normal height and stature. He stood rigid and statue-like, his eyes the only thing to betray his life force and energy. His eyes were oily black pools, slick and alert, darting around him and taking in the surroundings. His gaze fell upon his saviour and settled for a moment. The recognition was immediate and triumphant.

The two embraced and all fell silent. It was a sinister, menacing silence, heavy with dread and expectation. The birds fell silent and the air was thick with malevolence. The red walls of the abbey shuddered and resonated with an uneasy hum, protesting against this unnatural and sacrilegious reunion.

"Ambrose Steele, welcome! You are once more free. Free to avenge our family and complete our quest for power and treasure. Together we will be strong, we will be invincible... and will take back that which is ours by right and in time!"

On the hillside above, the dark magic had awoken three older and malevolent souls. The evil-doers awoke from their long sleep, cast into the sandstone, banished for an eternity to expiate their dreadful sin.

At the same instant a dart of lightening pain shot through the very hearts of Nate, Rob and Rebecca. They were alerted and uneasy, filled with dreadful anticipation, but as yet, not knowing why. They knew without speaking their thoughts that the last battle was joined and that they must face their old foes and vanquish or fade away themselves.

Afterword

In a different time, not so long ago, a young girl awoke abruptly. Today was going to be an important one. It was July, hot and sunny and it was her eleventh birthday. Her two best friends, Kevin and Susan were going to spend the day with her at Furness Abbey and take a picnic. They had been lots of times but today would be different. She could feel it in her bones-something exciting would happen today.

Just how exciting she would never have been able to guess…

Author's Note

The third novel in the *Out of Time* series is darker than the previous two. Again the action is concentrated around the small coastal town of Barrow-in-Furness and Furness Abbey. The times visited this time include the nineteenth century when Barrow was in its infancy. One of the new characters is Sir James Ramsden who is a particular hero of mine. He was one of the triumvirate of visionaries who took the tiny hamlet from obscurity to the forefront of the industrial revolution. He was an ideas man and worked in concert with industrialist H.W. Schneider and the Earl of Burlington – later the Duke of Devonshire, who provided the investment. Sir James became the town's first mayor and he is remembered by statues and street names in the town. He was knighted in 1872 and lived long enough to see Barrow become a Borough Council. His vision for the town included an Iron and Steel Works, which processed the iron ore that was mined locally. At one time the Bessemer Steel Works were world famous and this led to the establishment of the Shipbuilding industry. The town grew from 30 families to a population of 60,000 in just over forty years. It was an energetic and industrial town, nicknamed the 'Chicago of the North', referring to the lawlessness and mainly male dominated population. Ramsden attempted to ameliorate this by building a Jute and Flax Works to encourage a female workforce.

He interests me because he came from a fairly humble background and started out as a humble Locomotive Superintendent, but his rise was rapid. He was rewarded for his efforts by Furness Railway Company with a fine house, Abbotswood, built close by the abbey. He was allowed to rent it for his and his descendant's lifetimes and although it is long gone, the local memory remains.

When I was researching the earlier books, Ramsden's image kept popping up, in the Town Hall, the library and St George's church. I read a lot about him and found the story of his idea to save the company money by demolishing the abbey to make way for the railway. Something changed his mind and luckily it didn't happen, the engineer Mr McClean preferring to spend an extra £300 to blast a tunnel, thus avoiding the abbey. This set things in motion and Ramsden suddenly became completely intrinsic to the story.

The historical information is as accurate as I can make it, but I have taken a certain licence with anecdotal evidence and local stories. The story of the murder at the monastery arises from research from the Coucher Books written at the abbey by scribes, including the real John Stell. The late local historian Alice Leach told me about the story and we both thought it had to be written about. Sadly, Alice died this year but she leaves an amazing legacy of research and books as well as inspiring a generation of school children.

I must mention the real Furness Abbey "treasure" a

Bishop's golden crosier and ring, found in 2010. The local group of volunteers *Furness Abbey Fellowship* are now fully established and they have raised funds to purchase a special case for the artefacts to be on permanent display. This is an exciting time for the abbey and lots of events and activities are being provided in conjunction with FAF and English Heritage. There is now even an annual Medieval Fair on the last Saturday in August. I continue to promote the abbey through my books and make many visits to schools and with pupils to the abbey.

Again I have plundered my family history and although this is a work of fiction, I like to think that the essence of some of these people has been captured for posterity. The third book is darker and more sinister and this time ends with a cliffhanger. I make no apologies for this and the final story in the series will conclude the tale. I hope you enjoy this story as much as the others and that you take the opportunity to visit some of the amazing places in the wonderful Furness peninsula.

Gill Jepson

www.out-of-time.co.uk